STO

☞ P9-ECL-482

DISCARDED

DO NOT REMOVE
CARDS FROM POCKET

10-5-94

BILL BRITTAIN

SHAPE-CHANGER

HarperCollins*Publishers*

Shape-Changer
Copyright © 1994 by Bill Brittain

Library of Congress Cataloging-in-Publication Data
Brittain, Bill.
    Shape-changer / by Bill Brittain.
        p.   cm.
    Summary: Two seventh-grade friends help a shape-changing policeman from the
planet Rodinam as he tries to recapture an alien master criminal who can also
change form.
    ISBN 0-06-024238-8. — ISBN 0-06-024239-6 (lib. bdg.)
    [1. Science fiction.   2. Extraterrestrial beings—Fiction.]   I. Title.
PZ7.B78067Sh   1994   93-27268
[Fic]—dc20   CIP
                                                                              AC

Typography by Tom Starace
1   2   3   4   5   6   7   8   9   10
❖
First Edition

For the librarians—especially those
who deal with children.

Thank you and God bless you!

CHAPTER 1

THE BUMP IN THE NIGHT

In the beginning, I figured I had to be dreaming—or else my brain was turning into Silly Putty. There was that loud sound from the sky at three o'clock Monday morning, like a million people all humming on a kazoo at the same time. Then the light, so bright I had to squint just to look at it. Next, the bump that shook the whole house. And a patch of earth that had been turned into glass.

Crazy!

It wasn't until I had my little talk with the fire hydrant that things started to make sense.

I guess the best place to start is on Sunday afternoon. Dwight Hobisher, Lauren Kyle, and I were sitting on Dwight's front porch. All three of us were bored out of our socks.

"So why don't we go and play with the other kids?" I asked in my best Bill Cosby imitation.

"Because there *aren't* any other kids," replied Dwight and Lauren together. "Yak, yak, very funny."

It was a kind of joke we had about living in Rolling Acres.

Rolling Acres Estates is a couple of miles out of town, and there are only three houses here. Lauren's house is next to mine, and Dwight lives across the street. All the rest of the development is just big holes in the ground where other houses will be built some-day—maybe.

Oh sure, there's old Mr. Pixley's farmhouse and barn down the road a little way. But Mr. Pixley—he's the farmer who owned all the land before the devel-oper bought it—is mean and crotchety, and we try to keep out of his way as much as we can.

Dwight and Lauren and I are all in the same sev-enth grade class at Winslow Junior High School. Dwight's the really smart one, especially in current events. Maybe that's because his father works for the government and spends a lot of time in Washington.

Lauren Kyle's about eight inches taller than I am, but she's real nice to me anyway. She always calls me Frank instead of "Francis" or "Frank-the-Shrank," like a lot of the other kids at school.

Me? I'm Frank Dunn. If you ever need to find

me, just look for the shortest kid around. Mom and Dad say that in a few months I'll start growing like a weed, and I'll be as tall as anybody else in my grade. That's supposed to make me feel better.

It doesn't.

"We need something to do," I said with a sigh. "How about if we try to catch ourselves a squirrel? There's plenty of them around."

"No way," said Lauren. "I caught one once—in a net. When I went to take it out, it just about bit my finger off. Then I had to go to the doctor and get a shot with a needle. I learned not to mess with squirrels."

"If you guys want something to do," said Dwight, "figure out how I can get my folks to take me to Washington with them. Dad's working on a government contract, and he's taking Mom with him. Two weeks at the Federalist Hotel, with all expenses paid. I want to go too. Dad's all for it, but Mom says I'll miss too much school."

"Nag your mother," Lauren suggested. "Mope around a lot, and give out with long sighs. Cry real tears, if you have to."

"I've been doing that," said Dwight. "But Mom's on to all my tricks. And they're leaving tomorrow morning. Unless I can get her to agree to take me, I'll be stuck for two weeks with Mildew Beecham."

"Yecchhh!" Lauren and I moaned together.

Miss Mildred Beecham—we kids called her "Mildew" when nobody else could hear—had taken care of all of us at one time or another when our parents went away. Compared to Mildew, The Wicked Witch of the West was all sweetness and charm. Mildew made us brush our teeth after every meal. We had to do three hours of homework as soon as we got home from school, and she always had a list of jobs for us whenever we began watching TV.

A real pain. I hoped Dwight got to go to Washington. I didn't want Mildew Beecham anywhere near me—even across the street.

After what seemed like about a million years, that boring afternoon ended. I went home and cooked supper.

Yeah, I cook. Mom and Dad both work at the real estate office, and they expect me to help out. Actually, I'm a pretty good chef. Okay?

Later on, I climbed into bed and read the chapter on photosynthesis in my science book. It was the third reading, and I still couldn't even figure out what the word meant.

The afternoon had been boring.

The chapter was even more boring.

I fell asleep with the book still propped up on my stomach.

Suddenly my eyes popped open. The room was dark. The glowing hands of my alarm clock pointed to five minutes past three . . . in the morning. For a second, I couldn't figure out what woke me up.

mmmmmmmmmmmmmmmmmmmmmmmmmmm

I sat up in bed. The humming sound was coming from outside.

mmmmmmmmmmmmmmmmmmmmmmmmmmm

I tossed the blankets aside and hopped out of bed. The floor was cold against my bare feet.

I peered out of my bedroom window. Darkness, except for the stars and the crescent moon in the sky. Everything seemed to be the same as always.

Then . . .

mmmmmMMMMMMMMMMMMMMmmmmm

For just a second the sound got louder, like when you're standing at the edge of a road and a car passes. At the same time, the moon seemed to blink off and then on again. But that couldn't be . . .

. . . unless something had passed *between* me and the moon.

mmmmmmmmmmmmmmmmmmmmmmmmmmm

Suddenly, on top of the little hill behind our place, I saw the light. Something really weird was happening.

Hey, I've seen bright lights before. I've seen laser shows and searchlights and the flame from a welder's torch. But those were puny compared to that light on the hill. It seemed almost solid, a bar of brightness coming from up in the air down to the ground. Then . . .

MMMMMMMMMMMmmmmmmmmmmmmm. . . .

The light disappeared and the strange noise stopped. It got awful quiet. I shook my head and wondered if I was . . .

TTHHUUMMPP I could feel the whole house shake. It was like, out there in the darkness, a huge giant had slammed a great boulder—or even a small mountain—down onto the earth.

Then it was silent again.

For maybe thirty seconds I just stared out into the dark.

I'm no hero. But I had to find out what was going on out there.

I turned on the bedside lamp, put on my heavy bathrobe, and laced up my sneakers. Then I grabbed the big flashlight I used to read comics under the blankets when Mom and Dad thought I was sleeping. I opened the door of my room and tiptoed along the hallway.

There was no light under the door of my parents' room, and it was quiet inside. I guess they were sleeping through all the excitement.

I unlocked the front door, stepped out into the night, and began walking toward the hill where I'd seen the light. The earth and weeds on the ground were damp, and before long, water oozed through my sneakers. Once I stepped in a hole and nearly fell. Little insects kept flying through the flashlight beam.

Suddenly I heard a rustling sound, like something being dragged through the weeds—something heavy. I moved the flashlight in a circle all about me.

"Who . . . who's there?" I called in a shivery voice.

No answer. The rustling sound had stopped.

I was scared right down to my bones. But curiosity got the best of me. I kept walking up the hill instead of scurrying back home.

At the top, I aimed the flashlight all over. Weeds, a mud puddle, and the stump of a tree. I paced around in a big circle. Everything seemed normal. Off in the distance a bullfrog croaked a few times.

Then another sound came to my ears. It was a kind of crackling . . . or popping . . . something like radio static or paper being crumpled. But it was close by. And who'd be playing a radio or crumpling paper at this time of night? I kept really still, waiting for something else to happen.

Okay, I thought finally. Maybe the humming and the light and the big bump were just things I'd imagined. Maybe the rustling in the weeds and the pops and crackles meant nothing at all. I'd better get back to . . .

Clunk

My left foot came down on something hard. I tipped the light downward to see what I'd stepped on, expecting it'd be a chunk of wood or a rock or . . .

With eyes popping, I dropped down on my

hands and knees. I rubbed my fingertips along the surface of the ground, unable to believe what I was seeing or touching. Then I got up again and shined the light around the whole area.

There wasn't a weed or a pebble or even any dirt where I was standing. Instead, a big circle in the field, six or seven feet across, had all been turned into *glass*.

Even I know that melting dirt into glass takes heat—a lot of heat. The glass was still hot. The crackling, popping sound was made as it cooled. Around the circle's edges, the weeds were burned and charred.

I was scared! I peered into the darkness, half expecting something out there to attack me.

I ran down the hill. If I could just get inside my front door, I'd be safe. I got closer and closer when . . .

"Frank?"

My heart leaped in my chest like a yo-yo. Whatever kind of a thing it was, it knew my name.

"Frank? It's me. Lauren."

I pointed the flashlight toward the sound. Sure enough, there was Lauren, wearing a blue bathrobe and fuzzy rabbit slippers, standing at the doorway of her house.

"What are you doing up?" I demanded.

"Some kind of a bump in the night woke me," she said. "I was looking out to see . . ."

"There was more," I told her. "Didn't you hear the humming and see the light and . . . and . . ."

"Humming? Light? It sounds to me like you were having one of your nightmares, Frank. Just because there was a little earthquake or something, you don't have to . . ."

"It was no earthquake, Lauren. You just slept through the exciting part. Come on. I want to show you something."

"Really, Frank, I should get back to . . ."

"Oh no. You've got to see this." I took her arm and kind of dragged her back up the hill. When we got to the circle of glass, I flashed my light all over it.

"What do you think of that?" I asked.

Lauren knelt down and placed her fingertips on the surface of the glass. "Still warm," she said.

"So now you have to believe me—right?" I said.

"I believe this is glass," she replied. "And I can't explain how it got here. But what's that got to do with the humming and the lights you were talking about?"

"Don't you see, Lauren? It all goes together. It's one big mystery that . . ."

"There you go—imagining things again. Look, we're all bored, living out here in Rolling Acres. But I'm sure there's some perfectly logical explanation for this."

"Lauren, you didn't see and hear what I . . ."

"We'll talk about it in the morning, Frank."

"But . . ."

"I'm sure that tomorrow, you'll be a lot more sensible about this." She turned and started back down the hill. I went along, lighting the way for her.

I kept trying to get her to understand what I'd seen and heard. But she kept insisting there was some normal way to explain everything.

She went into her house, closed the door behind her, and locked it. I sneaked back to bed.

But I couldn't sleep. When Mom stuck her head into my room to call me, I was already wide awake.

Monday. School.

Lauren, Dwight, and I stood on the corner, waiting for the schoolbus. "So with the humming and the light and everything," I was saying, "I'm certain that . . ."

"You were dreaming, Frank," said Lauren.

"Oh yeah? Well how do you explain the glass?"

"Maybe the Rolling Acres workmen came out and did something," said Dwight glumly. "Do you have to make a big deal out of everything?"

"Workmen? In the middle of the night?"

"Who knows? I don't want to talk about it anymore. I've got problems of my own."

Every kid in Rolling Acres except me thought I was nuts. There really wasn't much more to say.

"What's bugging you, Dwight?" Lauren asked.

"Mom and Dad decided to go to Washington without me," he grumbled. "They left real early this morning, and when I woke up, there was the note, saying I should be good and do all my schoolwork."

"Gee, I'm sorry, Dwight," said Lauren.

"Now I'm stuck with ol' Mildew Beecham for two weeks. I'm her slave until my folks get back."

"Poor guy," said Lauren, patting him on the back.

So much for my big adventure, I thought. Dwight gets sympathy. I get treated like a nut case.

I really could have done without school that day. I was so tired I actually fell asleep in English class, and all the kids got a good laugh when the teacher woke me up. Then I got my science test back. D-.

During lunch, Zach Baylor and Cornelius Cobb caught me in a deserted corner of the second floor hallway. Zach's an eighth grader in Winslow Junior High School. He's tall, and he's got pimples on his face, and he just lives to make life miserable for anybody littler than he is. You know—the kind of guy who gives ordinary bullies a bad name.

Corny Cobb is built along the general lines of an interstate truck. His favorite pastimes are stomping ants, crushing flies, and slapping people around. Sure, that name of his is a natural for making jokes. But nobody—and I mean *nobody*—ever says those jokes out loud.

I was just pulling my math book out of my locker when I heard this voice behind me. "Well, if it ain't Frank-the-Shrank."

I looked around. There were Zach and Corny— and nobody else in sight. I was a goner.

"Now don't get all uptight, Frannnn-sis," Zach went on, dragging out my name like it was the funniest sound in the world. "We just wanna borrow some paper. Right, Corny?"

"Right, Zach." Corny snatched my notebook from under my arm. He yanked out a fistful of paper and threw the notebook into a corner. Then he pointed to my open locker.

"Get in, crumb-bum!"

I wasn't about to argue with Godzilla. I crammed myself into my locker. Zach slammed the door, trapping me inside.

"You know what's gonna happen if you tell anybody who done this," Zach whispered through the vent slots. "Just keep your mouth shut, Frank-the-Shrank."

Being in that locker was like wearing an iron straitjacket.

When the bell rang, the seventh graders came upstairs and I started shouting. Somebody let me out. Everybody laughed at me, for the second time that day.

Later, when we got off the schoolbus at Rolling

Acres, Dwight said he had to report to Mildew Beecham, who probably had a jillion jobs for him to do. Lauren was going shopping with her mother.

That left me alone.

I took a walk to the hill. Sure enough, there was the circle of glass. But in the daylight, it wasn't all that impressive. It had cracked into small pieces as it cooled, and it looked like someone had spread glass pebbles on the earth.

Next I went past the old Pixley farmhouse and barn. From the road—just a lane scraped by a bulldozer—I tried to peer into a window of the house. But all the curtains were closed tight. One of 'em moved a little, and I'll bet Mr. Pixley was inside peering back at me.

Further down the dirt road, I came to a hole that might—someday—be the foundation of a new house in Rolling Acres. I went over and sat down on a pile of cement blocks and stared into the hole. Maybe I was nuts, the way Lauren and Dwight thought. But I just couldn't get that circle of glass out of my mind.

"I think that . . . perhaps you can help me."

The words sounded like they were coming from an electric razor that had learned to talk. I looked around.

Nobody. Just me and the cement blocks and a few scraggly trees and a red-and-white fire hydrant sticking up from the ground near the dirt road. Unless someone was hiding behind a tree trunk, I was hearing things. And after last night, I . . .

"Do not look so . . . puzzled. I am right here . . . in plain sight."

In plain sight? But there was nothing . . .

"Turn your head this way. Please do not be afraid. I will not harm you."

That's when I saw it. Like I said, it was red and white, and it had a kind of valve thing on top, and two more on the sides, with chains hanging from them. It was almost like the ones I'd seen a thousand times in the village and never looked at twice because they were so common.

But whoever heard of a fire hydrant with a *mouth*?

A BLOB OF GRAY JELL-O

I had to be seeing things . . . and hearing things. I closed my eyes and grabbed my head with my hands.

I opened my eyes. The mouth was still there. The bright red lips moved stiffly.

"I have no intention of harming you, boy."

My eyes were bulging out of my head, and I was breathing hard. Even though the day was cool, I could feel sweat popping out all over me.

Dwight and Lauren were right, I thought to myself. I *am* crazy.

"You are the person who was walking about last night, are you not?" the lips went on.

If a fire hydrant could talk, who knew what else it might do? Somehow I had to get away.

"Yaaaaa!" With a loud scream, I sprang from the bench and began running toward home.

I didn't get far.

An arm—it was more like a tentacle—shot out of the side of the hydrant. It wrapped itself around my ankles and pulled tight. I fell down, hard. Lying on the ground with the tentacle still tying my legs together, I turned to face the hydrant.

"Have you lost the power of speech?" it asked.

"Please . . ." I began in a quavering voice. "Please let me go."

"I will release your legs only if you promise not to try to escape again. We have much to discuss, you and I."

"I . . . I promise. I'll be good. I'll do anything you ask."

"Very well." The tentacle loosened from around my ankles. But it remained poised to grab me again if I made a single false move.

"Now go back and sit on the bench."

"Yes, sir . . . or whatever you are." I sat down again. "Just don't hurt me."

"You're perfectly safe, as long as you make no further attempts to escape. In fact, I need you to help me with my mission."

"You want help . . . from me?" I said slowly.

"Indeed. But first, we need a more private place to talk. Where can we go?"

"I . . . I dunno."

"You must live somewhere. A house . . . an apartment . . . a condominium."

"I live in a house. But . . ."

"Take me there."

Great. A living fire hydrant wanted to go home with me. I shifted uneasily on the bench, and the tentacle grabbed my wrist.

"Look, I can't rip a fire hydrant out of the ground," I told it.

"I am not really a fire hydrant. I merely took this form when I saw several of these devices in the village this morning."

"Then what . . . what *are* you?"

"My name is Zymel. I am one of the Shilad."

"The what?"

"This is no place for questions, boy. We need privacy—now! Take me to your house before I'm forced to do something we'd both be sorry for."

"But how do I take a fire hydrant . . ."

All at once there was a *whish*ing sound. A stiff breeze blew against my face. It stung my eyes, and I closed them tight.

When I opened them again, the fire hydrant was gone.

Where it stood, a book lay on the ground. It had a green cover and appeared to be brand-new. I looked down at it. I was ready to move fast if the book grew a tentacle and attacked.

There was an odd design on the green cover. It

was almost like letters of the alphabet—but not quite. I bent down, picked the book up, and tried turning the pages.

I couldn't do it. The thing in my hand looked like a book, and it felt like a book. But when I tried to open it, I discovered it was one solid block of paper and cardboard.

Then, like something out of a movie cartoon, two rubbery lips appeared in the middle of the cover.

"Quickly now," said the lips. "To your house."

What could I do? If the thing could change from a hydrant to a book, it could just as easily become a man-eating tiger or a black widow spider. I shoved the book under my arm and ran toward my house as fast as I could. I scurried inside and set the "book" gently on the coffee table.

"Are we in a place where we cannot be observed or overheard?" the book asked.

"Ye . . . yeah. I guess so."

"Look around. Look carefully. Is there anything—anything at all—which you cannot remember being in this room before?"

I looked. Two chairs, a sofa, a couple of tables, and some crocks of plants in a corner of the front window.

"Everything's just like it's always been," I said. "But who—or what—are you? Am I really flipping out?"

"You are completely sane," snapped the book. "In the absence of a more competent entity, I have reluctantly chosen you to assist me."

"Assist you? What do you mean by that?"

"Before answering, I will assume my real form. Perhaps that will make it easier for you to understand what you are dealing with."

I heard the *whish*ing sound again. The breeze brushed my cheek. The book . . . changed!

On the coffee table was what looked like a blob of gray Jell-O, about as big as a loaf of bread. Inside the blob was a network of yellow veins. A single purple eye stared at me without blinking. Above the eye was a slash that had to be a mouth.

"That's better," said the mouth crisply. "Communication is *so* difficult when I'm in the form of an inanimate object."

"But who . . . what . . ."

"To repeat myself, my name is Zymel. At least, that is the closest I can come in your somewhat primitive language. And you are . . ."

"Francis . . . I mean, Frank Dunn. Just call me Frank."

"Very well, Frank. You are the one who came out to see where my spacecraft crashed last night, is that not correct?"

"Spacecraft? But . . ."

"Stop sputtering, Frank. We cannot waste time.

We have much work to do, you and I."

"Work? Hey, I don't even know . . ."

"Of all the life forms in the galaxy," grumbled Zymel, "I had to find one in whom curiosity outweighs good sense. Oh, very well, Frank. I will attempt to explain my appearance here as briefly as possible. I am one of the Shilad. We Shilad inhabit the planet Rodinam in the Loraa Star Cluster, which . . ."

"Shilad? Rodinam? Loraa Star Cluster? I don't . . ."

"Frank! If you keep interrupting, it will be too late to accomplish our task. Let's just say that my planet is farther away from here than you could ever imagine. But we have developed space vehicles which can transport us across whole galaxies in just a few of your Earth days."

I stood there with my mouth gaping open. This was *Star Trek* and *Return of the Jedi* and every sci-fi story I'd ever heard of, all in one. But it was real! And it was happening right there in my living room.

"You were a fire hydrant . . . then a book . . . then . . ."

"The Shilad are shape-changers," said Zymel impatiently. "We can assume any form we wish."

"*Any* form? You've got to be kidding."

"Oh? Really?"

Whish! The breeze fluttered the curtains at the windows.

On the coffee table where Zymel had been stood a ten-speed bicycle, all blue and gold, with black tires and shiny handlebars.

"Hey, be careful! If you scratch that table, Mom'll . . ."

Whish!

The bicycle was gone. In its place was a big green watermelon.

Whish!

A Raggedy Ann doll.

Whish!

A king-sized bottle of aspirin.

"Okay, okay!" I yelled. "I believe. You can do it. But how come you can speak English?"

Whish!

The gray blob reappeared. "On Rodinam, we study civilizations of other planets, much as you learn in school about other countries of this world," it said. "My area of specialty in . . . eh . . . college . . . was your solar system. I'm quite an authority on how you live here.

"In addition, I explored the business area of the nearby village this morning. People were about, purchasing food and other items. I listened to their talk, and also scanned a dictionary on a wire rack. I'm rather proud of how rapidly I learned your rudimentary language."

"The village? But didn't anybody notice you?"

"Who would look twice at a spotted dog or a shopping cart or a box of rubbish?"

My mind was trying hard to catch up with what I was seeing and hearing. "But what are you *doing* here? On Earth, I mean."

"At last," said Zymel with a sigh of relief, "I can come to the point. You and I must locate Fek quickly and . . ."

"Fek? What's a Fek?"

"Fek, like me, is a Shilad. And unless he is found soon . . ."

"Wait a minute. You mean there are *two* of you?"

"Quite so. And that is why I need your help, Frank Dunn."

"Zymel, I'm really confused."

"Must I explain everything in infinite detail?" snapped Zymel in annoyance. "Oh, very well. To begin with, on my planet I am what you would call a . . . a policeman. I was assigned to transport Fek across your solar system to prison, when . . ."

"You mean this Fek is a criminal?"

"Fek is a master criminal. But more than that, he is totally insane. Imagine, if you will, the ruthlessness of the great white shark . . . the deadliness of the cobra . . . the stealth of the stalking lion . . . the cruelty of a mad dog . . . and the intellect of the most gifted human. Then you have some small idea of the criminal who is Fek. The confusion and chaos and terror and bloodshed he and his shape-changing ability could bring to a planet such as this is impossible even to imagine.

"Fek was captured on Rodinam some time ago. He was placed in an ion cell, where shape changing is impossible. The cell was installed in my police craft, and I was assigned to bring him to some barren asteroid where he could do no harm."

"But something happened, huh?"

"Yes. The fuel cell of my spacecraft broke open. I began losing power to the rockets—and to the ion cell. I knew I had to make a landing. And since, in my studies, I had some knowledge of this . . . this Earth of yours and knew I could adapt to your atmosphere, I chose to set down here. Turning on my retro-blasters . . ."

"The loud humming!" I cried out. "That was . . ."

"My engines. And the blasters create a bright light and enough heat to . . ."

" . . . to melt dirt into glass," I said.

"Yes. Unfortunately the power ran out before the ship landed. We crashed to Earth. At the same time, Fek leaped from his damaged ion cell, changed into a Brakonian quark-beast, and attacked me. I, of course, countered by becoming a glyff worm and tried to wrap myself about him. Before I could, he seized me with one of his seven graspers and hurled me from the ship. I struck something hard and was rendered unconscious."

"So . . . so Fek has the ship to himself."

"Indeed. Frank, you observed my ship coming down. But did you see it take off again?"

I shook my head. "Except for that circle of glass, I didn't see or hear anything once the bright light went out. Wait. There was a sound—like something heavy being dragged through the weeds."

"Then it's as I suspected. The ship is too damaged to operate properly. Fek must have used the levitator to carry it off."

"What's a levitator?"

"A device for lifting and moving an inoperative spacecraft. With it, Fek could have carried the ship . . . oh . . . perhaps one of your Earth miles away."

"You mean Fek is somewhere within a mile of us right now?" A prickly feeling went up and down my backbone.

"Probably. At least the spacecraft is. Once the levitator runs out of power, the ship's weight makes movement impossible."

"You've gotta find him, Zymel."

"*We* must find him, Frank. If we fail, he may repair the ship and cruise about the galaxy, spreading evil wherever he goes. Worse yet, Fek may not succeed with the repairs."

"Wouldn't that be good? You'd have him trapped here on Earth."

"Yes," said Zymel with a sigh. "Trapped on Earth would be a mad killer with the power of assuming any shape it wishes. If he took the guise of your President, his every order would be obeyed. As an army general he would command the most fearsome of your weapons. We must find Fek at once—before he dooms your whole planet."

"But Zymel, how are you going to recognize Fek if he can take any shape at all?"

"His first instinct will be to repair the ship, if possible. If we can locate the spacecraft, we'll know that Fek is about somewhere. We'll simply wait for him. Then, once we overpower and capture him . . ."

Frankly, I wasn't too wild about the way Zymel tossed that word *we* around. "Shouldn't the police be told about this?" I asked. "Maybe the FBI or somebody?"

"That would be unwise, Frank. The more people who know of our search for Fek, the greater the chance of his learning our plans and taking measures against them. Also, we have little time—a week, at most—before Fek completes the repairs. Your police, with their silly guns and handcuffs and clubs, would only waste the few days we have."

"This ship—what does it look like?" I asked.

"It's a disk. In your crude measurements, it's about seven feet in diameter. Much wider in the center than at the edges."

"A regular flying saucer, huh? But seven feet wide? I was thinking of something bigger. Like the spaceship *Enterprise* on television. A seven-foot ship wouldn't be that hard to hide."

"We must find it, Frank. Fek must not be allowed to spread his terror throughout your world."

"I'd like to help you, Zymel," I told the blob. "I really would. But I've got to go to school. After school, I have homework. After homework . . ."

"School? Your whole planet is on the brink of disaster, and all you can think of is school?"

"Hey! You're the one who wanted to keep the search a secret. If I don't go to school and act as if things are normal around here, it'll look suspicious. People will start asking questions. And I'm not very good at lying."

"Hmmm. Very well, you will go to school as usual. As for the . . . the 'homework' . . . What are you studying?"

"In science, we're talking about something called photosynthesis," I said. "But it doesn't make much sense to me. I wish somebody'd explain it so I'd understand."

Zymel's single purple eye rolled upward. "Photosynthesis," he whispered. "What did the dictionary say? Ah, yes. The method by which plants . . ."

Suddenly the eyeball shifted and looked straight at me. "Lie down on the couch," Zymel ordered.

"Lie down? Why?"

"I need to probe your brain in order to give you

the necessary information about photosynthesis."

"My brain? Is this going to hurt?"

"Not at all. I will mount myself on your head. There will be no discomfort."

"Are you sure?"

"On Rodinam, we do it all the time. It's considered very impolite to refuse a brain probe."

Well, I couldn't be rude to a guest, could I? I lay down and stared at the ceiling. Zymel oozed his way down the leg of the coffee table, and a moment later I could feel him covering my head like a gelatin cap.

It didn't hurt, but it wasn't the most pleasant thing in the world, either, having the glop that was Zymel plastered on the top of my head.

All of a sudden there was a picture. I wasn't seeing it with my eyes, but with my brain. I was four months old and sucking milk from a bottle. Then . . . my third birthday, when the big present was a jack-in-the-box . . . the first day of kindergarten . . . joining the cub scouts . . .

Then, in big black letters flashing on and off:

PHOTOSYNTHESIS

It was like watching a cartoon. Yellow lines of sunlight came down on a leaf. Inside the leaf, green cells used the sun to help make food.

Five seconds of that show inside my head and I knew more about photosynthesis than I'd found out from all the science books I'd ever read.

Zymel oozed off my head and down onto the floor.

"So *that's* how it works," I said. "It's so easy."

"Yes," Zymel said. "And while I was in your mind, I copied the contents of your brain into my own system."

"You did *what?*"

"I now know every fact you ever learned, every emotion you ever experienced, every idea, every . . ."

"Those are my private property!" I howled. "You can't . . ."

"It was necessary, Frank. I had to be sure you were not Fek in a changed form—or someone who would be likely to help him. I also need to learn more about your human ways of thinking."

"Oh sure! You got what you want. But what about me? You took my . . . my soul, almost. Of all the dirty tricks. . . ."

"I do apologize, Frank. But . . ."

"But, nothing! From now on you keep your jelly body and your tentacles and all that stuff to yourself. If you want entertainment, go read a book. But stay out of my head, or . . ."

Suddenly the front door burst open. In walked Lauren Kyle.

"I was coming over to help you with your homework," she said. "I heard you talking with somebody and . . ."

She looked around the living room. I was the only human there. Then she spotted the gray blob on the rug. "Frank, what's that mess?"

And Zymel picked that moment to talk.

The slash of mouth opened. "Who is this girl?" the blob asked in a loud voice. The single eye glittered ominously.

"Ohhhh." A little moan came from Lauren's lips. Her face turned a pasty white. "It . . . it looks like something a plumber might take out of a clogged drain," she whispered. "But it talks. Frank, is this a joke you're pulling on me?"

"No joke," I said. "Lauren, this is Zymel."

"I told you it's not wise for another human to know about me," said Zymel. "If Fek should . . ."

"She's already seen you," I snapped. "What do you want me to do, lock her in the closet for the rest of the week?"

"But . . ."

"Look, you talking blob of gray bubble gum. I've already said I'll help you if I can. But for now, you just shut your . . . your face while I explain a few things to Lauren!"

CHAPTER 3

NEW GIRL IN SCHOOL

I helped Lauren to a chair and began talking. Explaining Zymel to Lauren was harder than I'd thought it would be. I'd start in about how Zymel had been taking a criminal to prison in his rocket ship, and Lauren would just stare at the gray blob and mutter, "I'm seeing things . . . none of this is real . . ." and stuff like that.

It was even worse when I got to the part about shape changing and Zymel demonstrated by turning into a lawn mower and a marble statue of a horse and *Webster's Unabridged Dictionary.* Lauren would cover her eyes and then peek and start moaning about how she was going crazy.

Then I had an idea. "Lauren likes kittens," I told Zymel. "Can you change into one?"

Whish!

The orange-and-black-striped kitten tottered across the rug and rubbed its fuzzy body against Lauren's leg. "Oh!" she cried. "It's so cute."

Gingerly she picked up the kitten—Zymel—set it in her lap, and began petting it. Suddenly she looked at me suspiciously. "This kitten isn't going to change into that gray glop, is it?"

"No," I said. "At least I don't think so."

Holding the kitten, Lauren listened really carefully as I told her about Zymel and Fek and how the flying saucer was stolen away after it had crashed. Sure, the whole thing was hard to believe. But she'd seen Zymel and heard the bump in the night. Lauren's no dummy. She realized that weird things were going on in Rolling Acres.

"Okay, so you're looking for a spaceship," she said when I'd finished, "and another gloppy thing named Fek. But Frank, there's something about this Fek that you haven't thought about."

"I've already explained to Frank that Fek is a cruel, merciless killer," said the kitten. "He seeks power and will do anything to obtain it. What more could I tell?"

"If I was Fek," Lauren replied, "and I knew you were looking for me, I wouldn't just sit around waiting for you to show up."

"What do you mean?" I asked.

"Fek's a slimeball, all right. But you said he's real smart, too. Now if you're being chased, the smart thing might be to get rid of whoever's doing the chasing."

I didn't like the sound of that at all. "You . . . you mean that while we're going after Fek, he might be coming after . . . *us?*"

"It makes sense, doesn't it? He could be in this room right now, getting ready to cut our throats."

I glared at the kitten. "Zymel, why didn't you tell me . . ."

"I thought you understood the peril, Frank," the kitten replied.

"But I don't want to . . ."

"Too late, Frank," said Zymel. "We're all in danger now. Fek is capable of killing anybody he even *thinks* knows about him."

"And we can't even hide," I wailed. "Tomorrow we have to go to school. Otherwise Fek—wherever he is and whatever shape he's taken—would be really suspicious."

"What'll you be doing, Zymel?" Lauren asked. "Prowling around the neighborhood?"

"No. I will stay with you and do my best to protect you."

"But kittens don't go to school," said Lauren.

"Then I will take another form." The kitten hopped to the floor. "Frank," it said, "get a coat from the closet there. Cover me with it."

I hauled out Dad's old raincoat. As I put it over the kitten, I couldn't help wondering what shape Zymel had decided on.

The Wolfman?

The Creature from the Black Lagoon?

The slimy being from *Alien*?

It had to be something so horrible and monstrous it would scare Lauren and me silly. Otherwise, why the raincoat? Zymel hadn't needed a cover when he'd changed shape before. Why now?

Whish! The coat suddenly rose up as if pulled by a string from above.

The thing, about as tall as I was, stood there with its back to me. When it turned around, the coat was buttoned from top to bottom. The head was all I could see.

That hair, all around the face . . . those big eyes, blinking at me . . . those white teeth, grinning . . . Oh, no!

"A girl!" I howled. "You're gonna be a *girl* when we go to school?"

"What better shape, Frank?" Now Zymel even had a girl's voice. "In human form, I can visit your classes without attracting attention."

"But how am I going to explain having a girl with me?" I asked. "Especially one nobody's ever seen before?"

"I leave that to you and Lauren," it—*she*—said. "First, though, I'll need a name."

"Dream up your own name."

"Hmmm. Let me consult the thoughts I read in your brain. Dolly Parton? Meryl Streep? Oprah Winfrey, perhaps?"

"Try something else, Zymel."

"Queen Victoria . . . Martha Washington . . . Calamity Jane . . ."

"Those are from the history books. Keep it simple."

"How about Mary?" Lauren suggested.

"Fine," said Zymel. "And a last name?"

"Well, you're from a place far away. Why not . . . Farr?"

"Mary Farr," said the "girl." "I like that. Am I pretty, Frank?"

"Well, uhhh . . ."

"You look fine, Mary," said Lauren. "Frank just doesn't know how to handle himself around girls."

Okay, Mary Farr was cute enough. But no way was I going to tell this thing which was really a gray blob that she was . . .

"You can't go to school in my father's raincoat," I said.

"I've already got that worked out," Lauren told me. "Tonight, Zymel, you can be a kitten and stay under our porch. Tomorrow when you're a girl again, I'll lend you some of my clothes to wear."

"Thank you, Lauren," said "Mary" with a little giggle.

Just then I heard the sound of a car pulling into our driveway.

"My parents are home," I sputtered nervously. *Whish!*

The raincoat collapsed to the floor. The orange-and-black kitten crawled out from under it.

Lauren picked up the kitten and tucked it under her arm. She reached the front door just as Mom and Dad walked into the living room.

"No, Frank," said Lauren, "you can't possibly wear that raincoat. It's much too big for you. And don't leave it on the floor. Hang it back in the closet where it belongs."

She looked at my mother and shook her head. "Boys!" she exclaimed with a sigh of exasperation.

The kitten under her arm purred loudly as Lauren opened the door and walked out of the house.

Just as I was about to close the door behind her, I noticed a great, black dog, almost as large as a small pony, sitting in Dwight Hobisher's front yard.

But Dwight didn't own a dog.

And the animal seemed to be watching Lauren intently as she made her way across the lawn.

Was it just a stray dog, or was it . . .

I kept the door open until Lauren was safely inside her own house.

———

There's a schoolbus stop down at the end of our street. On Tuesday morning, I was the first one there. I darted glances around at the trees and the rocks of Rolling Acres. Any of them could be Fek, the interplanetary madman, waiting in ambush.

A few minutes later, I saw Lauren coming toward me with Mary Farr beside her. Mary had on a plaid skirt and a green sweater. "At first my shoes didn't fit her," Lauren told me. "But Zy . . . I mean Mary . . . kind of adjusted her feet, and now everything's just fine."

Those two chattered away, with Zymel sounding like a real girl.

A few minutes later, Dwight Hobisher came out of his house, carrying his book bag.

"Not a word to him about the spacecraft or our search . . . or anything!" Mary whispered to me.

"But Dwight's our friend," I said. "And besides, he already knows Lauren and I heard and saw those screwy things the night you landed."

"Don't question my orders, Frank. When Lauren discovered my mission, she thought she was going insane. I won't go through that again. As we agreed, just pretend I'm a girl who's visiting here."

I introduced "Mary Farr" as my cousin from Minneapolis. Dwight's usually a charmer with the girls, but he still seemed pretty glum about not going to Washington.

"Maybe after school, we could all take a walk around the neighborhood, Dwight," I suggested. "We could . . . uh . . . check up on anything new, that we haven't seen before."

I thought I was being real clever.

Mary Farr kicked me on the leg—hard. "After school, *we* have to search alone!" she whispered in my ear.

"Mildew won't let me go," Dwight told us. "And if you even come by, she'll probably put you to work, too. Boy, do I wish I was in Washington instead of waiting for the dumb schoolbus."

The schoolbus showed up, and all the kids greeted the new girl, Mary Farr. As long as nobody called Mom or Dad at their office, things would be just fine.

At school, we got off the bus and walked into the building. Students mobbed the halls, locker doors were slamming open and shut, and everybody was yelling at one another while a couple of teachers on hall duty tried to keep some kind of order.

I was surprised to see how frightened Mary Farr looked. "This is madness, Frank," she said in a quivering voice. "So much noise."

What? Was the great Zymel chickening out because of a little screaming and shouting? I was getting worried that Mary Farr would blow her cover and change back into the gray blob. That'd be all I needed with so many students and teachers around.

"Stay cool, Mary," I said. "Remember, you're just visiting."

The attendance office bought my story about my cousin visiting from Minneapolis and handed Mary a pass, good for the whole week. We went to homeroom and from there to first period.

Math.

Ms. Hughes, our teacher, wrote out a problem that took two blackboards. "Solve that," she ordered. "It shouldn't take more than ten minutes."

Ten minutes? I didn't even know how to get started. I looked around and saw that most of the other students were in the same boat.

"The answer," I heard Mary murmur into my ear, "is eleven."

"I know you're a visitor," Ms. Hughes said, pointing at Mary, "but we do not whisper in this class. What was it you told Frank?"

"I'm sorry I whispered," Mary replied. "I just told him the answer was eleven."

"But in a few seconds you couldn't possibly have . . ."

"Oh, it's quite simple. By using a base 6 reference and Arvinian Star Cluster logic, one can easily see that . . ."

"Please do not make jokes at my expense, young

lady," said Ms. Hughes sternly.

"But . . ."

"Not another word. I think you need lessons in good manners more than you need them in math."

While all this was going on, Lauren just sat at her desk with her hand over her mouth, choking back her laughter. I wanted to give her a good swift kick.

After math class, Mary Farr decided to keep her mouth shut for the rest of the morning.

At noon, in the cafeteria, I asked Mary if her new form could handle human food. She said she thought so, and I bought her lunch. It was goulash—the kind of school lunch that can rot your stomach.

As soon as I set the plate down, Mary began forking that stuff into her mouth like it was chocolate pudding. "Good," she said between big bites.

There's no accounting for the tastes of space aliens.

After scraping the plate clean, Mary wanted to look around the school. Most of the kids went outside when they'd finished eating, and we had the halls to ourselves.

Well . . . almost to ourselves. We'd just passed the science lab on the second floor when . . .

"Hey, look, Corny. Frank-the-Shrank has got himself a cute li'l lady friend."

Zach Baylor and Corny Cobb were standing there and blocking the hall. Just what I didn't need right then.

I tried an end run, but Corny grabbed my shirt and hauled me back again. Then those two goons herded Mary and me into a corner.

"Ain'tcha gonna introduce us to the pretty girl?" sneered Zach.

"My name is Mary Farr," she told them as if she were really the Queen of England in disguise. "Now if you two animals will just get out of my way . . ."

"Listen to her!" Zach cried out. "She talks like we're a couple of slimeballs. That's not polite, honey."

"If you don't move aside," Mary said, "I will not be responsible for the consequences."

"Oh, la-de-da," sneered Zach. "Little Miss Prim and Proper. Be nice to us, sweetie."

Corny reached out and pinched Mary's cheek.

"Very well, if that's how you intend to act. But don't say I didn't warn you."

"Warn us about wh . . ."

RRRIIIPPP

With a loud tearing sound, the right sleeve of Mary Farr's blouse burst apart. And suddenly her right arm wasn't that of a twelve-year-old girl anymore. Instead, the arm was long and huge and hairy, and it had big muscles that would have made Arnold Schwarzenegger jealous.

Zach and Corny were staring at the arm, just like I was. The hand clenched into a fist. The arm moved backward and then forward like the piston of a steam engine.

The fist caught Corny Cobb right in the chest. Corny, big as he was, went flying across the hall and banged into the lockers with a loud crash. He slumped to the floor.

Mary's massive hand grabbed the front of Zach's shirt, lifted him into the air, and shook him like a baby's rattle. I could hear Zach's teeth clicking as his head bounced around on his shoulders.

"You just tell me when you've had enough of this," said Mary in her sweetest voice as she continued to rattle Zach's brain.

"E . . . E . . . Enough!" Zach finally managed to cry out.

"Say please."

"P . . . P . . . Please!"

The great arm lowered Zach to the floor. Over by the lockers, Corny Cobb started to get to his feet.

"You'd better stay right where you are, if you know what's good for you," Mary told him.

Corny stayed right where he was.

As Mary Farr and I walked around the corner of the hall, her great arm shrank back to girl-size. She looked around, suspiciously. "I'm sorry that had to happen," she said. "I let my temper get the best of me."

"Hey, I thought you were terrific!"

"No, Frank. If Fek is about, he now knows about my disguise. But we know nothing of his. In this building, every student, every teacher, even every book, could be our enemy."

I hadn't thought about that. I couldn't help wondering if the trash can down the hall would suddenly attack me.

Somehow we got through the rest of the school day. By the time the buses came, I was a nervous wreck. Could the bus itself be Fek? If so, he could run us into the river and drown us without even trying.

When we got off the bus at Rolling Acres, Dwight ran off ahead of Lauren and Mary and me. "Mildew Beecham has really got him scared," I said as we trudged down the dirt road.

We'd just turned a sharp curve in the path when Mary suddenly stopped. Lauren and I watched as she turned her head from side to side. "I hear something," Mary said.

Then I could hear it, too. It was the hoofbeats of a horse . . . a horse that was running fast.

But there weren't any horses around Rolling Acres.

The hoofbeats got louder . . . louder . . .

Suddenly the mystery horse leaped out of the trees and onto the path right in front of us.

It was huge, with great hoofs that pounded onto the earth as it raced toward us. It tossed its head, and its nostrils flared, and eyes that were red with hate glared at us.

Lauren and I lurched to one side of the path. Mary threw herself to the other side.

The horse swerved toward Mary.

I lunged across the path, grabbed Mary's arm, and yanked her to one side. The horse raced past, its huge hoofs pounding down only inches from our heads.

Then it was gone, around the curve in the path. The hoofbeats faded into silence as quickly as they had begun.

Mary got to her feet. Both she and I were trembling all over.

"Where d'you suppose a horse could have . . ." I began. But Mary shook her head.

"That wasn't a real horse. It was Fek. I'm sure of it. Did you see how, when we separated, he lunged at me?"

Lauren and I looked at one another. All at once I realized that our talk about getting killed was more than just talk.

"But shouldn't we go after him?" I asked.

"No," said Mary. "By this time, he's a stone or a leaf or some other common object. We'd never find him. But it does mean Fek has seen through my human disguise. So . . ."

Whish!

A gray squirrel hopped away from a pile of clothing on the path. The squirrel waited while Lauren stuffed the clothes into her book bag.

When Mom and Dad got home, I was in my room, pretending I was doing my homework. I couldn't let them see how scared I was. They'd have wanted to know why. And I didn't have any explanation that wouldn't make me sound like I was crazy.

That evening after supper, Lauren and I and a little squirrel took a walk through Rolling Acres. We were supposed to be looking for anything out of the ordinary.

I was also looking to keep from getting killed.

Nothing happened. Everything seemed the way it should be.

But in my imagination, I kept hearing the sound of a horse's hoofs, pounding toward us along a narrow path.

CHAPTER 4

SUSPICIONS

The next morning, after Mom and Dad had left for their office, I looked around for Zymel.

I checked out the whole house and finally ended up back in the kitchen. It was kind of eerie. Zymel could be anything. The coffeepot. The milk bottle.

Anything.

Why didn't he *say* something?

Finally I went outside. Lauren was waiting for me.

"Where's Zymel?" she asked. "Is he one of those pens in your pocket, maybe? Or . . ."

"He's just gone," I said. "I don't know where."

"Gone?" Lauren repeated.

"Yeah. And I'm kind of wondering, Lauren. Are we really sure that story about searching for Fek is really true? Oh, sure, a spacecraft came down, and Zymel got out of it. But Fek? Maybe Zymel himself is the bad guy. Maybe Fek doesn't even exist."

"But Frank—what about the horse yesterday?"

"So it was a horse. But was it really a space monster? Maybe it's just a nag that came unhitched from a hay wagon somewhere. All we've got is Zymel's story. And now he's disappeared."

The more I thought about Zymel, the angrier I got. I'd done everything I could to help that gray blob, and now he'd up and left. I'd never see him again. Of all the ungrateful . . .

Across the street, the door to Dwight Hobisher's house burst open. We could hear Mildew Beecham and Dwight shouting at one another.

"You will *not* play with your friends after school, young man! You will come right home and . . ."

"Come on, Mrs. Beecham. Give me a break."

"A break? That's the trouble with you young people today. You want . . ."

Suddenly Dwight came running out. He slammed the door behind him.

"I don't know how much more of her I can stand," he said as he trotted toward us. "And my folks won't be back at least until the weekend— maybe longer. I never saw anybody as mean as . . ."

"Calm down," I told Dwight. "Sooner or later she'll be gone, and things'll get back to normal."

Normal? Hah! If Dwight only knew about Zymel.

School that day was kind of a blur. All the questions I had about Zymel were really bugging me. I got angrier and angrier as I ticked them off in my mind.

Where was he?

Why did he leave?

Was he really a policeman, or . . .

By the time Lauren and I got off the schoolbus and were walking down the path toward home, I was so angry I was practically spitting nails.

"Zymel made suckers out of us," I said as we reached my house. "He said that . . ."

As I was going through all the things that made me angry, I unlocked the front door and walked into the living room . . .

. . . and there was Zymel—the hunk of gray gelatin—sitting on the coffee table.

"Where have you been off to, you talking lump of axle grease?" I demanded.

Lauren peered in through the doorway. "Frank, maybe you'd better calm down and . . ."

"No! How do we know he's telling the truth? If Zymel's really a policeman looking for a criminal, let him give me some proof."

"Fair enough," said Zymel. "Your newspaper is right there on the couch. Look at the front page."

I looked.

There were two stories about local events. *BREAK-IN AT FUEL DEALER* read one headline.

The other said: *SMITHSON JEWELERS ROBBED.*
I started reading the first story out loud.

> *"A hole was kicked in the rear door of Beck-ley Coal and Oil, Inc., late last night, and a per-son or persons entered the building. Although there was nearly a hundred dollars in an un-locked desk drawer, the only items missing were two bags of anthracite coal. Police are . . ."*

"That's enough, Frank," said Zymel. "Now the other one."

> *"Smithson's Jewelry Store had its front win-dow smashed yesterday, sometime after closing. A diamond ring and two diamond bracelets were taken. Four large ruby pins and a massive emer-ald brooch were ignored by the robber, who . . ."*

"There's your proof, Frank," said Zymel. "Proof that Fek is doing his best to repair the spacecraft be-fore I can find where he's hiding."

"You're going to have to do better than that, Zymel," I scoffed. "Some nut makes off with a cou-ple of bags of coal to keep warm this winter, and a jewelry store gets robbed, and I'm supposed to be-lieve that Fek is . . . What do you take me for?"

"Consider, Frank—the basic element from which

my ship's fuel is obtained is carbon."

I was all set to tell Zymel to take a long running jump in the lake. Then I noticed Lauren. She was staring at Zymel with her mouth open and her eyes wide.

"Fek didn't want money or rubies or emeralds," she said slowly. "Only coal and diamonds. Because coal and diamonds are both forms of . . . of carbon."

"Carbon? Where did you find out about . . ."

"In science, Frank. Last year. You remember, don't you?"

When it came to science, I couldn't even remember the name of the textbook. What a brain Lauren had.

"But . . . are you saying you believe Zymel now?" I asked her.

"It's the only thing that makes sense. Fek needs carbon for . . . for the ship."

"To fabricate fuel," added Zymel.

"I'm still not sure . . ."

"Come on, Frank," said Lauren. "You wanted proof that Fek really exists, and you got it, right in the newspaper. How else do you explain those screwy robberies?"

"Well . . ." Okay, it was beginning to look like Zymel had been telling the truth. "But where were you hiding before school?"

"I spent last night exploring the whole Rolling

Acres Estates," said Zymel. "At first that shack where the builders store their equipment looked promising."

"Yeah," I said. "It's big enough to . . ."

"Changing into a tiny spider," said Zymel with a sigh, "I crawled through the keyhole. Nothing in there except lumber and a few rusty tools. But . . ."

"But what?"

"Then I saw the barn."

"Mr. Pixley's barn—of course!" Lauren cried out. "It's been there since Rolling Acres was just farmland."

"Fek has to be hidden there with the ship," said Zymel. "I'm certain of it."

"What makes you so sure?" I asked.

"For one thing, the barn seems to be the only logical hiding place. All the other buildings—the houses—hereabouts are occupied. And besides that, while I was exploring, I came close to the barn and . . . and . . ."

"And what, Zymel?" I asked impatiently.

"I heard something moving around inside. There were footsteps and . . ."

". . . and you sneaked inside the barn," said Lauren. "Right, Zymel?"

"No, I did not. You see, there was an incident."

"An incident?"

"Yes. I was in my squirrel form, and I was standing beneath one of the outside lights over there, considering what my next move would be. Just then, a man came out of the house and onto the porch."

"Did he have gray hair and a big mustache?" I asked.

"He did indeed."

"That'd be Mr. Pixley."

"Your Mr. Pixley had a rifle in his hand. And he fired it at me!"

"Oh, dear!" Lauren cried out.

"He missed. But as I hurried away, I heard your Mr. Pixley say, 'Well, critter, you escaped the stewpot this time. But I'll get you yet. You just wait and see.'"

"Stew-pot," gasped Lauren. "You mean he wanted to . . . to *eat* you?"

I tried hard to keep from laughing. The idea of old Mr. Pixley having a space creature for supper seemed kind of funny somehow.

"I fail to see the humor in this," said Zymel. "To go on, however, I felt certain that the shot would have alerted Fek inside the barn. Regardless of what disguise I assumed, it was impossible to continue my detective work without serious risk of discovery. I didn't want to endanger you, Frank, by returning here, since Fek might follow me. So I hid out in the woods until after you'd left for school this morning."

"So what happens now?" I asked Zymel.

"If Fek *is* in the barn, he will be telling himself that Mr. Pixley's shot was just an occurrence and not a threat to him. He will let down his guard. So tonight is the time we must return."

"And what if the shot scared Fek so much he decides to move out?" Lauren wanted to know.

"He may leave. But he cannot take the spaceship with him. And if we find the ship, we have only to wait until Fek himself returns to it. By going back to the barn tonight, we have everything to gain and nothing to lose."

Nothing except my life, I thought glumly. "I dunno, Zymel," I said. "It sounds dangerous. And my folks aren't too crazy about my roaming around Rolling Acres after dark."

"That goes for me, too," added Lauren.

"I have told you the kind of being Fek is," said Zymel slowly. "If we do not accomplish our mission tonight, you may spend the rest of your lives—short though they may be—looking back over your shoulders at something that will be coming after you. It may be a horse, as it was yesterday. It may be a quark-beast or even some more unspeakable creature. But unless Fek is destroyed or captured, he will, in some form, come for you. Depend on it."

I looked at Lauren. She looked back at me. We were both shivering with fear.

"I . . . I guess we don't have any other choice but

to go to the barn with Zymel," I told her.

"I . . . I guess you're right," she replied.

That evening, I got in bed fully dressed and pulled the blankets up to my neck. I turned off my bedroom light about ten thirty. In about another hour, Dad started snoring. He and Mom never heard me raise the window in my room and hop out into the night.

Lauren was waiting for me. She'd brought a flashlight.

Standing beside her was a great, fuzzy St. Bernard dog. "I hope that's you, Zymel," I said.

"It is, indeed," said the dog with a wave of its front paw. "If anybody spots us, you two are just taking me for a walk. Now then, are you both ready?"

"Yes," said Lauren and I together. I hoped Zymel couldn't sense how scared I was.

We headed down the road toward the Pixley farm. Somewhere off in the darkness a cat yowled.

At least, I hoped it was just a cat.

CHAPTER 5

RAID ON THE OLD BARN

The St. Bernard and Lauren and I walked silently toward the Pixley farm. Every now and then Lauren would flick the flashlight on for a second or so, to keep us from getting lost.

There was a light in one window of the farmhouse. Inside, we could see Mr. Pixley, rocking back and forth in his chair.

"You two stay here," Zymel ordered. "I'm going to take a closer look."

The St. Bernard disappeared into the darkness.

"Zymel's good," said Lauren in a whisper. "Even with all those leaves on the ground, I can hardly hear him moving."

"Yeah," I answered. "Uhhh—Lauren?"

"What?"

"You didn't say anything to Zymel about me thinking he was . . . I mean . . ."

"About how he might be a criminal himself? Naw, I wouldn't do that."

"Being a cop where he comes from must be some job. With all that changing, you'd never know what you were looking for."

"Hey—there he is." Lauren pointed toward the house.

By the light from the window, I could see the dog crawling on its belly up to the house. It stood up on its hind legs and peered inside.

"We have to be careful," said Zymel when he returned. "Mr. Pixley's cleaning that rifle of his. We don't want him to come out and start shooting."

We circled the house and groped our way toward the barn. We didn't dare use the flashlight, and we couldn't see a thing.

"We're quite near the barn now," Zymel told us. I guess along with everything else, he could see in the dark. "Stay here. I'm going to scout around a bit."

He left us there in the darkness. But within a couple of minutes he was back. "The windows of the barn are all covered," said the St. Bernard, "but I was able to see through a crack. There are lights on inside."

"Is Fek in there?" I asked.

"I don't know. But where else could he be hiding?" the dog replied.

"So what do we do now?"

"We want to surprise Fek, so going in the front way is impossible. Those big doors are locked. But around in back is a smaller door, and the wood around it is half rotten. A single hard shove should break it. At my signal, both of you will slam your bodies against the small door, as hard as you can. As you crash through, I'll race past you and try to capture Fek."

"It sounds like a good plan, Zymel," I told the dog.

"However," he went on ominously, "it's a dangerous one."

"What dangers?" Lauren and I asked together.

"I believe that if you two can clear the way for me, I can subdue Fek before he has time to change his shape," said Zymel. "However, I can't be completely sure. There may be a fight between Fek and me. If so, you will see us assume different shapes, and at times I may seem to be losing. You are to ignore any seeming weakness on my part, and do not be astonished by whatever you may think you see. Stay clear of us. Your very lives may depend on it. Simply be there to warn me if anyone—or any*thing*—comes to Fek's aid."

I didn't want to be a hero. I told Zymel I'd follow his orders to the letter.

So did Lauren.

We sneaked to the rear of the barn. Lauren and I faced the door and kind of hunched our shoulders.

"Now!" barked Zymel.

I plunged toward the door. Lauren was right beside me.

CRASH!

Our shoulders both struck the door at the same time. It fell inward, and we fell right on top of it. We squinted at the bright light in the barn. At the same time I felt the paws of a dog running over me. There were a couple of loud barks followed by Zymel's shout: "Show yourself, Fek! Show yourself and surrender!"

Then the lights went out.

Lauren and I got to our feet. Everything was silent. We didn't know whether to remain still or run away.

I was all for running.

We heard Zymel's voice.

"It . . . it isn't here."

"What isn't?" I called.

"The spacecraft. I don't see it anywhere."

Lauren turned on her flashlight. She moved the beam about the barn. A spaceship—even a small one—would have been easy to spot. But Zymel was right.

No spacecraft.

At first glance, the place looked like the inside of any old barn. The floor was wooden planks with big gaps between them. In one corner was a pile of dusty crates and bags. Big, hand-hewn beams held up the walls and roof.

But at one side of the barn was a brand-new metal desk with a big lamp attached to it. On the desk was a computer, complete with keyboard and screen. The computer was surrounded by maps and notebooks. Behind the desk, two metal chairs had been tipped over.

There wasn't a speck of dust on any of the equipment.

"This barn had been electrified only recently," said Zymel. Lauren played her light on the new wiring that ran along the wall. "But I don't see how even Fek could have . . ."

"Hold it right there, both of you!" called a stern voice from the darkness. "One move, and I shoot."

A sound of footsteps. A click. The desk lamp and two others hanging from the ceiling blazed with light.

Out of a dark corner came a tall, skinny man in a plaid shirt and gray pants. Right behind him was his partner, short and fat and wearing a green sweatsuit. The tall man peered over black-rimmed glasses, and the little one was as bald as a billiard ball. They could have been a great comedy team.

Except they were both holding pistols.

"Okay, okay," snapped the tall one. "Hands over your heads. Don't make a move."

"We—we're not moving," I stuttered.

"They're just kids, Harvey," said the short one.

"Yeah, yeah, I see that, Max. But how about the dog?"

I glanced at Zymel. He was wagging his tail and looking friendly.

"But I could have sworn I heard the dog talking."

"Yeah, it sounded like that to me, too. But dogs don't talk, Harvey."

"Yeah, it had to be the boy and the girl here. So what were you two kids looking for?"

I looked at Lauren. She looked at me. I knew we were both thinking the same thing.

What should we tell these guys?

"We're looking for a big blob of gray Jell-O," I blurted out.

Both Harvey and Max stared at me like I was crazy.

"It's not really gray Jell-O," I went on. "It's a kind of space monster. And it can change its shape any-time it wants to and . . ."

"Kid, you've been watching too much television," said Max with a shake of his head.

In spite of the guns, I kind of chuckled to myself. How clever can you get? Fek would have been suspicious of me. These guys weren't. So chances were, they didn't know anything about shape-changers.

I glanced toward the St. Bernard. It was grinning and showing lots of teeth, and it nodded like it was real proud of me.

"What's goin' on out here?"

At the sound of the new voice, all of us—including the St. Bernard—turned toward the smashed doorway.

There stood Mr. Pixley with his rifle clutched in his hands.

"You said nobody'd disturb us here in your barn, Mr. Pixley," said Harvey. "But these two kids broke in and . . ."

"If you U.S. gov'ment fellas are gonna be sneaking around here with your top secret machines and stuff, you gotta expect folks to be curious," Mr. Pixley replied. "Now my barn door's been broke. If the U.S. gov'ment rents my barn, the U.S. gov'ment pays for my busted door."

"But it was these two kids and their dog who broke it."

"Kids and dogs ain't got no money. But the U.S. gov'ment has got all kinds of money. An' now some of it's owed to me."

"D'you know these two, Mr. Pixley?" Max was pointing at Lauren and me.

"Yep. Lauren Kyle's the girl. The boy's Frank

Dunn. They live just down the road a piece."

"We'll take 'em home," said Harvey.

"Nobody moves until my door's paid for."

"Tomorrow we can give you a payment order and . . ."

"Don't believe in them things. Cash on the table is my motto."

The two men looked at one another. Max, the short one, shrugged. Harvey, the tall one, reached for his wallet and began counting out bills.

"We're with SPONGE," Max began.

"And we're out a hundred and seventeen dollars," Harvey added glumly.

We were all in my living room. Lauren was on the couch between her parents, who'd come over as soon as Max had phoned them. I was standing, with Mom on one side and Dad on the other. Both parents were looking daggers at me. Max sat in the big easy chair, and Harvey had the smaller one.

The only person missing—if you could call him a person—was Zymel. Somehow, on the way home, our "dog" had managed to get himself lost.

"SPONGE?" Mom said to Max. "What's that?"

"Star and Planet Observation—National Government Effort," Max answered.

"Never heard of it," said Lauren's father.

"It's a government agency, sir," Max told him.

"Our job is to investigate any situations where we believe creatures from space might be trying to contact our planet."

"Our observation satellite indicated a possible landing of a strange craft near here Sunday night," added Harvey. "We were sent to investigate. We rented Mr. Pixley's barn for a few days and set up our instruments."

"A strange craft," said Dad slowly. "And it landed, and the little green men who got out had three toes on each eyebrow, I'll bet. Just what kind of a dope do you take me for?"

He turned to Mom. "Is our tax money really spent for such nonsense?"

"I know it sounds hard to believe, sir."

"Hard?" said Dad. "It's impossible! Look, I'll agree that Frank and Lauren shouldn't have broken into the barn. But when I think of you two guys sitting out here in the middle of nowhere with all your expensive equipment, and all you've got to show for it is two scared kids . . ."

"There was a dog, too, sir," said Max.

"A dog?" echoed Mrs. Kyle. "But there aren't any dogs in Rolling Acres. Lauren, what's this all about?"

"Some mutt followed us to the barn," Lauren said. "I don't know who it belongs to."

Nice going, Lauren, I thought.

Then Dad asked the hard question.

"What were you two kids doing out there, breaking into Mr. Pixley's barn?"

"Errrrr . . ." I began with my usual brilliance.

Just then there was a loud knocking at the front door. Mom went to open it.

The man she led back into the living room wore a wool overcoat of black and gray checks. His shirt was wrinkled and stained, his shoes hadn't seen polish in years, and on his head was a dented black derby. He looked like he'd just stepped out of a cement mixer.

"Gilroy's the name," he said in a harsh voice. "Oscar Gilroy, of the FBI."

"The FBI!" Dad exclaimed. "In those crazy clothes?"

"I'm in disguise," said Gilroy. "In the FBI, we use disguises like this all the time."

"First SPONGE, and now the FBI," Dad moaned. "When you kids get in trouble, you *really* get in trouble."

Gilroy stared hard at Max and Harvey. "What are you guys doing here?" he growled. "Why aren't you back at the barn?"

"What business is it of yours?" said Max. "We never saw you before."

"Of course you didn't. The FBI keeps its operations a secret. Not like you screwballs at SPONGE. Well, we're taking over now. And you two guys are in big trouble."

"But . . ." Max began. Gilroy scowled at Harvey

and Max like he wanted to eat them alive. "Are you gonna argue with the FBI?"

"N-no, sir," said Max.

"Now get back and haul that stuff out of the barn. I'll handle things here."

"Yes, sir. Right away, sir."

Both SPONGE agents sprang to their feet. They raced toward the front door. We heard it slam behind them.

"I don't want you parents getting upset," said Gilroy. "Frank and Lauren here aren't in any trouble. In fact they did us a favor by showing how weak the SPONGE security system is. But now the FBI is on the job, and everything is okay."

The strange man kept on talking. All four parents were shaking their heads in confusion. Gilroy did his best to calm them down.

Finally he stuck out a hand for me to shake.

I took the hand.

I was holding it when it changed.

The thing I held wasn't a hand anymore. It was the paw of a dog. Then, just as quickly, the paw was a hand again.

He shook hands with Lauren. A look of surprise flashed across her face. But with his back to our parents, Gilroy put a finger to his lips in a sign for silence.

We both knew what was happening.

Gilroy was Zymel.

"I understand your two men were carrying guns," Mom said to Gil—er—Zymel.

"Guns?" Mrs. Kyle looked shocked. "Those men had guns?"

"Yes, ma'am," said Zymel.

"They pointed guns at my daughter?"

"Yes, ma'am."

"Oh, my poor darling," said Mrs. Kyle, hugging Lauren to her. "I've heard quite enough, Mr. Gilroy. I find the actions of those men most irresponsible."

"Yes, ma'am. We'll see it doesn't happen again."

"I do hope so, Mr. Gilroy."

Zymel shook hands with our parents. After bidding everyone good-night, he went outside.

Lauren and I glanced at each other. She'd felt the hairy paw, too. We could hardly keep from laughing.

Good old Zymel. We should have known he wouldn't let us down.

Well, we weren't quite home free. Mr. and Mrs. Kyle turned to Lauren.

Mom and Dad stared straight at me as if they were trying to bore holes in my chest with their eyes.

"Now, young lady . . ."

"Now, young man . . ."

No television for a month. No more allowance forever. We were to come straight home from school every day and do our homework right away and obey every order our parents gave us, and keep our shoes polished and our room straightened up without being reminded all the time and do good works for the poor and never drop rubbish in a public place or spit on the street, and become model citizens who would make our mothers and fathers proud, and if we did all this, maybe . . . just maybe . . . on our fiftieth birthdays they would forgive us.

The usual stuff.

It was nearly two in the morning when the Kyles left and I got to go to bed.

I lay in the darkness, talking to a model of Lindbergh's plane *The Spirit of St. Louis*, which sat on a bookshelf. It was a really neat model. Better than anything I'd ever made.

"Zymel," I whispered to the plane, "it's a good thing you came back as Mr. Gilroy and got us out of trouble. But where did you get those screwy clothes?"

"They were in a closet in Mr. Pixley's house. I took them while he was in the barn. I knew they weren't suitable. But they were all I could find."

"I thought you were going to let Lauren and me take the rap all by ourselves."

"No, Frank. You got me into the barn. Even though we didn't find Fek, you and Lauren carried out all my orders. On the police force, a captain always takes care of the cops who work for him."

"The cops. D'you mean Lauren and me are like real police?"

"That's exactly what I mean. You're not only brave, you're extremely clever. If you'd allowed Max and Harvey to find out about me, any further investigation by us could have become extremely messy or even impossible.

"Back when I became the fire hydrant and first contacted you, I wished you were more grown-up. But now I think you two are about the best officers I've ever worked with."

I felt just as proud as if Zymel had pinned a medal on my chest.

But there was still work to be done.

"Where *is* Fek?" I asked.

"I don't know," said the plane. "And I'm very concerned. Obviously, neither Fek nor the spacecraft were in Mr. Pixley's barn. But where else could they be? Even with the levitator, Fek couldn't have moved the craft more than a mile from its landing site. It has to be somewhere nearby. And our time is running out."

"What should we do next, Zymel?"

"I don't know that either, Frank. I just don't know. And I'm afraid."

"Afraid of Fek?"

"Afraid of the awful things Fek will do to you and Lauren if he's not captured."

FEK

"I don't know where Fek is. I tell you, Frank, I've just run out of ideas."

"But you can't do that, Zymel. You're . . . like . . . the boss. You have to have a plan. You can't give up."

"But I can't think of anyplace here in Rolling Acres where Fek could be hiding."

I'd been having this same argument with *The Spirit of St. Louis* since an hour before my alarm went off. Sure, I understood that even Earth police sometimes get stuck on a case.

But if Zymel got stuck, I could get killed. So I couldn't let him just give up.

"Before I leave for school, Zymel," I said, "I want to know what your plans are for today."

"I'm going with you. If I can't find where Fek is hiding, the least I can do is protect you from harm."

"Zymel, I'm not carrying an airplane to . . ."

Whish!

A green book lay on my bed.

I crammed it way down in the bottom of my book bag. Then I got dressed and went into the kitchen.

Mom and Dad were still angry about last night. "You come right home after school," Mom ordered.

"And don't plan on going out again," Dad added.

"Sure, sure," I promised. I'd have promised them anything just to get them off my back.

When I came out of the house, Lauren and Dwight were waiting in the middle of the dirt road.

"Boy, I never thought I'd be glad for the chance to go to school," Dwight was saying. "But at least it gets me away from ol' Mildew Beecham for a few hours."

"I'm getting sick of your griping," Lauren told him as we set out for the bus stop at the end of the road. "We've all had to put up with her. We know what she's like."

Lauren looked beat. I guess I did, too. We'd both been up really late.

Suddenly something popped into my head. I reached way down into my bag, dragged Zymel out, and placed him on top of all my real books. I wanted him to be able to hear everything.

"Dwight," I said, "you really seem to hate

Mildew. Even more than the last time she took care of you. Is there something . . . uh . . . different about her now?"

Dwight thought about this. "No, I guess not," he said finally. "She's about as rotten as ever."

"She's in your house all day, isn't she?" I went on. "She even sleeps there."

"Come on, Frank," Lauren pleaded. "Give the questions a rest."

"And when you're at school, Mildew is all alone," I persisted.

"Well . . . yeah, but . . ."

Fek, I was thinking, could change into *anything*. Even ol' Mildew Beecham.

"Look, I'm sick of talking about Mildew!" Dwight snapped suddenly. "I'm sorry I brought the subject up."

But there was one more thing I had to find out. If Mildew was really Fek, then the spacecraft had to be hidden in Dwight's garage. It was the only logical place.

"I'll bet Mildew doesn't even let you go in your garage," I said to Dwight. "I mean, with your father's tools in there and everything."

"Are you kidding? The garage is the one place I can get away from her. She hates it in there."

That stopped me cold. If Dwight hid out from Mildew in the garage, there's no way he could overlook a spaceship seven feet wide.

"I said I was sick of talking about Mildew," Dwight said. "Let's change the subject."

Okay, she might have been weird, but Mildew Beecham had to be human. She wasn't our fugitive shape-changer.

In school that day, Zymel made me look good in both science and math. Nobody thought to ask why I was holding that green book up to the side of my head while Zymel whispered answers in my ear.

"Remember our lesson, Frank. During photosynthesis, oxygen is released into the atmosphere," he'd say softly.

Or: "If A is the base of the triangle, and B is its height, then A times B divided by 2 is the area."

I'd raise my hand and repeat what Zymel had said. The teachers thought I'd suddenly become a genius.

I began thinking there might be worse things than having Zymel trapped on Earth. Of course it might look a little screwy, me walking around school with a book plastered against my ear all the time.

During lunch, Zach Baylor and Corny Cobb walked over to me in the cafeteria. They herded me into a corner where they could hide me with their bodies.

"Where's your girlfriend with the great big arm today?" sneered Zach.

"She . . . she was just visiting," I said. "She had to go home."

"Awww, too bad." Corny had a big grin on his face. "That leaves you all alone, don't it, Frank-the-Shrank?"

"With just the two of us to protect you," added Zach.

At that, Corny made a grab for the books under my arm. Two of them fell to the floor. The one he picked up was green. Corny tried to flick at the pages with a dirty finger.

"Hey, Zach, look here," Corny said. "This book's all solid. It don't . . ."

That's when a mouth suddenly appeared on the book's front cover. The mouth opened, showing sharp white teeth.

The teeth clamped down on Corny Cobb's thumb.

"OOOOOWWW!" he screamed, dropping the book.

"Pipe down!" Zach ordered. "D'you want every teacher in the building to . . ."

"The book bit me!"

"Yeah, sure," replied Zach sarcastically. "If you don't watch them books, they'll get you every time. Books don't bite, you jerk."

"Look, my thumb's bleeding."

"Hey, Frank-the-Shrank, did you bite my buddy? 'Cause if you did, I'm gonna . . ."

"Okay, okay, what's going on here?" Mr. Lewison, the gym teacher, suddenly appeared behind Zach and Corny. He slapped a beefy hand on the shoulder of each one. "Are you two still picking on the little guys? Go on, get lost."

Zach and Corny got lost. But as they backed away, Zach pointed a finger at me like a pistol.

"We'll get you yet, Frank-the-Shrank," he snarled.

Right after lunch was English class. Ms. Boddicker was going to show a movie.

At least that was the plan.

The projector was all set up in the rear of the room. Ms. Boddicker reached up and grabbed the cord of the movie screen on the wall.

The screen unrolled like a window shade. When it was down, she let go of the cord.

ZIP! WHAM!

The screen snapped back up and slammed into its metal case. A couple of kids in the class giggled. Ms. Boddicker gave them a look that would have boiled eggs. She tried again.

ZIP! WHAM!

The screen sizzled up the wall again.

Ralph Keiser, who's in the AV Club, tried to help. He pulled the cord.

ZIP! WHAM!

ZIP! WHAM!

"Do you want me to get Mr. Follett?" Ralph asked.

Mr. Follett, the oldest of our school custodians, is a real Mr. Fixit. There's nothing he can't repair.

"Frank Dunn, you go," said Ms. Boddicker. "I need Ralph to run the projector."

I left the room, hoping Zymel would behave himself while I was gone. Down in the basement, I headed for the custodian shop.

Mr. Follett was standing behind one of the benches, busily cramming some wrenches, hacksaws, and files into a metal box.

He looked up and saw me.

"Whaddaya want, kid?" he growled.

That wasn't like Mr. Follett at all. He knew me. He knew all the students. Sometimes he called me Frank, and sometimes Francis.

But never "kid."

I came closer.

Mr. Follett wasn't wearing his usual uniform. He had on a leather jacket.

Well, maybe he'd ripped his shirt or had a little chill or something.

He kept looking at me angrily as he shoved more tools into the box.

"I said, whaddaya want?"

I told him about the movie screen.

"Not now. I'll do it later."

"But . . ."

"I said later, Frank-the-Shrank!"

Something was really wrong!

Mr. Follett never said a mean word to anybody. But here he was, calling me by that nickname I hated worse than anything in the world.

I walked around the end of the bench. I could see Mr. Follett from head to toe.

His feet were bare.

A leather jacket and bare feet? Either Mr. Follett was sick in some way or . . . or . . .

. . . this was *not* Mr. Follett.

I had found Fek.

I backed up toward the shop's door and my eyes were glued to those bare feet.

"Why are you staring, Frank-the-Shrank? Something wrong with my feet?"

"I have to . . ."

"Come back here, you little . . ."

Whish!

The thing at the bench wasn't Mr. Follett anymore. It was a huge, hairy creature like nothing I'd ever seen. Two great red eyes glittered in the middle of its chest, below a mouth filled with yellow fangs.

"Don't you touch me, Fek!"

"So, you know my name. What else do you know?"

If the thing grabbed me, I was done for. I shoved a big sheet of plywood toward it.

The plywood fell hard against the hairy thing's side. Fek toppled to the floor. I dashed for the door.

Whish!

From under the plywood crawled an insect nearly three feet long. It had steel-blue wings and antennae covered with yellow hairs. Its mandibles snapped open and shut menacingly, like huge pliers.

The thing came closer. Closer. I kept backing away until I felt the wall at my back.

Closer.

I looked around for some kind of weapon. There was nothing. All the tools were on the bench or in racks across the room.

The only thing near me was a wooden box full of sawdust. I picked up a handful and threw it at the awful bug.

The sawdust scattered and covered the thing's moist, bulging eyes. It screeched in surprise and pain. For a moment it was blinded. It staggered about, clawing at its eyes with its front legs.

I had to escape now.

I put a foot against the creature's side and pushed as hard as I could. The insect flipped up . . . and over. It lay on its back, struggling to right itself.

As I sprang for the door, one black leg brushed my ankle.

I yanked open the door and dove through it, out into the hallway. The door swung shut behind me.

From inside the shop I heard a sound like claws ripping along the panels of the door.

Then . . . silence.

Something touched my shoulder. I almost fainted from fright.

I turned around. There was Mr. Follett, wearing his blue uniform.

"I was working down the hall, Francis," he said. "I heard you scream. What's the matter?"

He gripped the doorknob.

"Don't!" I cried out. "It will . . ."

Mr. Follett pulled the door open and peered inside. Then he turned and looked at me.

"I don't see anything, Francis."

Terrified, I looked into the shop. There was no sign of the awful creature that had attacked me.

Fek had to be hiding. But where? He could be a bench or a tool or a piece of lumber or even a pile of sawdust.

Two teachers came running up. "What happened?" one of them asked.

What could I say? Who—besides Zymel—would believe me? I had to get back to him as quickly as I could.

With my heart pounding like a jackhammer, I made up a story about being frightened by a big spider in the shop. I even managed to smile.

The teachers laughed at me and told Mr. Follett to take me back to class.

All the way up those long stairways, I looked closely at every locker door . . . every drinking fountain . . . every ceiling tile . . .

. . . every doorknob, every window, every radiator, every scrap of paper.

I tried to remember which ones I'd seen before and which ones were new to me.

Because any one of them could be Fek, just waiting for his chance to attack.

CHAPTER 7

THE SMARTEST DOG THAT EVER WAS

"Obviously, Fek was gathering tools for his work on the spacecraft," said *The Spirit of St. Louis*. "He took Mr. Follett's form to be less conspicuous."

Lauren and I had just gotten home from school and were in the living room at my house. I was still frightened that Fek might show up again.

The model plane that was Zymel sat on the coffee table.

"You were wise, Frank, not to tell anyone at school of your encounter with Fek," Zymel went on.

"They'd have thought I was nuts!" I said. "But I've never been so scared in my life."

"And with good reason. Given the opportunity,

Fek would have killed you without a second thought in order to keep his own presence a secret."

"But why would Fek come to our school?" Lauren asked. "There are stores and factories and a lot of places where he could get tools."

"I don't know," said Zymel. "However, the fact is that Fek's repairs to the ship must be approaching completion. In another day or two at most, he will be ready to make his escape. Somehow, he must be prevented."

"But how, Zymel?" asked Lauren. "Here it is Thursday, and we're no closer to finding Fek than we ever were."

"I agree," said Zymel. "Further searching is useless. We must remember, however, that Fek knows as little of our plans as we do of his. Perhaps he will panic. Or he may become overconfident and therefore careless enough that we can discover his whereabouts. In any event, we must not give up hope."

"But it doesn't look good," I said mournfully. "Does it, Zymel?"

"No, Frank. It does not."

There wasn't much more to be said. I put *The Spirit of St. Louis* back on the shelf in my room. Then I asked Lauren if I could come over to her house for a while. After my meeting with Fek, I didn't want to stay home by myself—or even talk with Zymel—until my parents arrived.

"Sure," said Lauren. "We can study . . . or just talk, if that's what you want."

We put on our coats and walked outside. I slammed the front door behind me.

We walked out to the dirt road . . .

. . . and that's when Zach Baylor and Corny Cobb came racing up on their bicycles. They circled us. Lauren and I had to stop or else get run down.

Zach and Corny braked their bikes. "We figured you'd be coming outside sometime," drawled Zach with a mean grin. "All we had to do was wait long enough. And here you are."

"What are you guys doing way out here?" Lauren asked.

"We came to have it out with Frank-the-Shrank," Corny told her. "We don't like what he's been doing to us in school."

"I didn't . . ." I began.

"That Mary Farr had a punch like gettin' kicked by a mule," said Zach. "And then Corny's sure one of your books bit him. There's something strange goin' on, Frank-the-Shrank."

"Now's our time to get even," Corny added.

"My dad and mom will . . ." Lauren began.

"Your folks are out shopping," said Zach. "And Frankie's mama and papa are hard at work in the village. There's nobody around except us. Or maybe you think ol' Mildew Beecham across the street is gonna let Dwight come and rescue you."

I knew that would never happen. Mildew didn't care what happened outside. She just didn't want dirt tracked on the rug.

"This is my home, Zach," I said, almost pleading. "You can't just come out here and . . ."

"And what, Frank-the-Shrank?" Zach replied. "I ain't gonna do nothing to you."

"We ain't gonna touch you," Corny put in.

"Then what . . ."

Without a word, Zach twisted up his mouth so that his lower lip touched his upper teeth. He took a deep breath—and blew.

A high, shrill whistle came from Zach Baylor's mouth. It echoed from the rocks and trees of Rolling Acres.

Out of a small grove of trees came the dog.

Short, powerful legs pushed the muscular body like a railroad engine getting up steam. The snakish head, too large for the rest of the animal, had eyes like slits cut in a piece of furry cloth, and the mouth was full of long, pointed teeth. It was the perfect pet for somebody like Zach. Mean, clear through.

The animal growled as it padded—or waddled— to where Zach was standing. It looked up at its master as if waiting for orders.

Lauren and I were too scared to do anything but stare at the dog. First Fek and now this dog. What next? Dracula and his dragon?

"Sit, Ripper," Zach commanded.

The dog sat.

Ripper. What a name. Already I could imagine myself being chewed up into chopped meat.

"My dog," Zach told us proudly. "I trained it myself. It'll do anything I say. Watch."

He pointed a finger at the animal and then at Lauren and me. "Ripper . . . guard!"

The dog turned toward us and growled deep down in its throat.

"Oh, Frank!" gasped Lauren.

I was just as worried as she was. I didn't want to get munched up like an Oreo cookie.

"You're really safe," said Zach. "Just don't make any sudden moves. Ripper won't attack unless I tell him to."

Then Zach turned to Corny. "Find a stick," he said.

Corny located a piece of a dead tree limb at the edge of the road. He handed it to Zach.

Zach pulled back his arm. He threw the stick as far as he could. "Ripper. Fetch!" he snapped.

The dog raced to the spot where the stick lay. Big teeth clamped onto the wood. Then Ripper came back, holding the stick in its mouth.

Big deal, I thought. Any dog can be trained to fetch and . . .

"Ripper. Kill!"

Okay, you can't kill a stick. But that dog sure

tried. It ground the wood in its mouth, and I could hear the crackling and popping as Ripper's teeth made toothpicks out of the limb. I couldn't help imagining what the animal would do to my bones if it ever got the chance.

Zach and Corny were having the time of their lives. They knew how scared I was. "Lemme show you something else," said Zach. "Corny, hold out your arm."

Corny Cobb's arm, stuck out stiffly from his shoulder, had to be almost five feet off the ground.

"Jump, Ripper!"

The dog took a couple of steps forward and then jumped. Up it went, like an Olympic star.

It cleared the arm by at least six inches.

"Y'see," Zach told us, "wherever you go, Ripper can follow. So don't get any wise ideas about escaping, because my dog will do anything I tell it to. And . . ."

Slam!

I knew that sound. It was the front door of my house. Hey, maybe I'd got lucky and my folks had come home early. Maybe . . .

I looked over at the door.

The thing that had opened the door—and closed it—was a gigantic wolflike creature almost the size of a pony. Its shaggy coat was black and gray, and as it opened a mouth that seemed almost as big as our garage door, great fangs, nearly as long as my thumbs, glittered in the light.

Both Lauren and I breathed sighs of relief. It was Zymel. It had to be. He'd seen us from the window and . . .

"What . . . what's that?" Zach gasped. He and Corny stared at the great beast, and their eyes were about popping out of their heads.

"That?" I said with a chuckle. "Oh, that's my dog, Zach."

"That's a dog?" whispered Corny Cobb. "Not even lions are that big. Zach, maybe we should . . ."

"Yeah." Zach and Corny began backing off down the road. After one glance at the monstrous Zymel, Ripper put its tail between its legs and followed them.

"Zymel . . . guard!" I cried out.

The great wolflike thing galloped ahead of the fleeing bullies, who came to a quick halt. Zymel stood there, his four legs spread wide and the hair on his back standing straight up.

Corny Cobb tried to edge around Zymel. Zymel growled threateningly and bared his teeth.

Corny froze, looking like a big, dumb statue.

"My dog eats other dogs for lunch," I told Zach. "Sometimes he munches people for dessert."

At that, Zymel turned his dog's head and gave me a look that showed he understood what a liar I was.

But I couldn't help it. I was having fun.

"Just . . . just let us go, Frank-the . . . I mean, Frank." Zach looked like he was going to start crying. "We won't ever get on your case again. I promise."

"Well . . . maybe I'll let you live this time," I replied. "But you know, Zach, you seemed kind of proud of what you trained Ripper to do. Just wait till you see Zymel. He's the smartest dog that ever was."

I snapped my fingers. "Zymel! Come here."

Neither Zach nor Corny moved an inch as the great dog left them and walked over to me.

I pointed to a pool of muddy water at the edge of the road, about a hundred yards away. "Zymel, I want you to go down to that puddle. Walk there on your hind legs. When you get there, write my name in the mud. Be sure and spell it right. Then you're to bark twice and return to me. On the way back you'll walk on your front paws. Have you got that?"

"Hey, Frank!" Zach exploded. "There's no animal in the world that can . . ."

His voice faded away. Both he and Corny watched in amazement as Zymel rose up on the dog's hind legs. It walked off down the street until it came to the puddle.

Zymel stuck out his paw and began scratching in the mud.

"Arf . . . arf!"

He had to try three times before he could get up on his front paws. But he finally made it, with his head hanging down. He staggered his way back to where Lauren and I were standing and lowered himself onto all four paws.

Zach and Corny just gaped at one another as if they couldn't believe their eyes. "It ain't possible," I heard Corny whisper.

But I wasn't quite done yet. "Zymel," I said, "I told you to write my name in the mud. Did you print it instead?"

The huge dog did its best to look ashamed. Then it nodded its head slowly.

"Bad dog. Go back and fix it, right now!"

Zymel trotted off down the road. When it got to the muddy area, it brushed away the letters it had printed. Then, with great swipes of its huge paw, it began writing.

"I don't believe . . ." Zach began. All at once he ran down the road toward the puddle. Corny was close behind him.

"Jeez, look!"

Lauren and I strolled after them and stared at where Zach was pointing.

F-r-a-n-k. The scrawled letters were crude but readable.

"Poor handwriting," I said. "My dog will have to practice."

I don't think Zach and Corny heard me. They were already on their bikes and pedaling off as fast as they could. The dog Ripper scuttled after them, its short legs racing like pinwheels.

I patted Zymel on his huge, furry head. "Thanks," I told him. "I think that'll take care of those two. They'll be scared of my dog all through high school."

"You're quite welcome, Frank," the dog replied. "I didn't feel I should stand by and let those two push you around. If we're all finished, however, I'll go back inside where I can return to being an airplane. I find this canine disguise both uncomfortable and ridiculous."

That night, after I'd gone to bed, *The Spirit of St. Louis* and I were whispering in the darkness.

"Are you sure your room door is locked?" the airplane asked. "And the window, as well?"

"Just the way you wanted it," I said. "But we never locked up before. What's so special about tonight?"

"I've been wide awake for the past week," Zymel replied. "But like you, Frank, I require a dormant period from time to time. I'm exhausted and need a trance state to refresh myself. It wouldn't do to have Fek sneaking in on you when I'm not on guard."

"Trance state? D'you mean like sleep?"

"Yes—but much deeper slumber than you experience. Somewhat like . . . oh . . . a bear, hibernating for the winter."

"You're going to sleep all winter?"

"Of course not. A few hours should do me nicely."

"But what if Fek does get in here somehow?"

"It's difficult to awaken us Shilad from a trance state until we're ready. But it can be done. If you feel there's any threat to us, you must shout, as loudly as you can. I will hear and regain consciousness. I hate to do this now, when time is so precious. But I am so tired . . . very tired."

Zymel's voice trailed off. A few moments later I heard a sound like a cricket's chirping and water gurgling through a pipe and radio static, all at once. But it wasn't very loud, and I wondered where it was coming from.

I put my ear next to the fuselage of *The Spirit of St. Louis.* Then I knew.

Zymel was snoring.

The clock on my dresser ticked another minute away.

I stared at the clock for almost an hour before falling asleep myself.

In my dream I was a little baby, lying on Mom's lap and waving my arms and legs and grinning happily up at her smiling face. Then I was five years old, and we were in a store, and Dad was buying me a playsuit with a yellow duck on the shirt. After that, we were going on vacation, and I had the back seat of the old car all to myself and I was hugging a big panda bear that I could hardly get my pudgy arms around.

When I woke up, it was nearly three o'clock.

I sensed something . . . different. It took me a few seconds to realize what it was.

My head was covered with what felt like a gelatin cap. All at once I remembered the day I'd brought Zymel home.

I didn't know why he was giving me another brain probe. We'd been together all week, and he knew everything I did.

The probe felt strange, but not uncomfortable.

"Zymel?" I said.

"Not finished yet," said a voice inside my head. "More time. More time."

"Well, just find out what you need. No getting into my private thoughts like you did last time."

I kept my head still. But my eyes darted around the room.

From what I could see in the moonlight coming through the window, everything seemed to be in order. The chair and desk where I did my homework. The dresser where my clothes were kept, the mirror above it, the closed closet door and the shelves full of books and souvenirs, and *The Spirit of St. Louis* that was really . . .

. . . Zymel. His cricket chirp–gurgling water–radio static snoring came softly to my ears.

But if Zymel was on the shelf, then who . . . or what . . .

I put my hand on top of my head. It landed on a soft, sticky thing that felt like library paste.

I felt the thing ooze away from under my hand. I heard it slithering down the bedpost.

Suddenly I knew it was only by the luckiest chance I'd woken up and interrupted the brain probe.

The probe was *not* being done by Zymel.

It was Fek.

That's when I screamed. And screamed. And screamed.

CHAPTER 8

DUEL

"Fek was here, Zymel! He was inside my head!"

"Trying to find out what we've discovered about him, no doubt," said *The Spirit of St. Louis*. "But I hear your parents coming, Frank. You must not tell them of my existence—or of Fek's."

Dad and Mom burst into my room and rushed to the side of my bed. "You were screaming loud enough to wake the dead," said Dad. "What happened?"

"It . . . it . . ." I looked toward the shelf where *The Spirit of St. Louis* sat. The plane's propeller was spinning slowly around.

"It was just a bad dream," I told my parents. "I guess I shouldn't have had that second dish of ice cream before I went to bed."

The worried looks vanished from Mom's and Dad's faces. They smiled at one another.

"Tomorrow's a school day," said Mom. "You'd better get back to sleep."

"Sure, Mom. Sure."

But I knew there wouldn't be any sleep for me the rest of that night.

My parents left, turning off the light. For several minutes there was nothing but silence. Then . . .

"Frank?"

"Yeah, Zymel?"

"You're frightened, aren't you?"

"You bet I am. In five days, we haven't found out where Fek hid the ship, or what he's up to or . . . or anything. But he did his best to kill me in the school shop, and tonight he came right into my house and perched on my head. I wish Fek would get his ship repaired and fly away from here. I really do."

"That would be a disaster."

"I don't care. Just let the disaster happen somewhere else. I've had enough. I don't want to be mixed up in this thing anymore."

"But you are in it, Frank. Just as I am. I'm convinced that before leaving this world, Fek will do his best to kill us both. His sick mind wants revenge for the trouble we've caused him."

"Kill?" I said with a gulp. "You mean after he did the brain probe, Fek might have . . . have murdered me?"

"Indeed. I suspect you discovered him and raised

the alarm just in time. But Frank, I will do my best to protect you."

"Up to now, your best hasn't been all that good, Zymel. You're a cop, but you don't have a clue as to where Fek is. So how can you . . ."

"You'll be safe enough for the rest of the night. I will remain on guard. But can't we continue this discussion in the morning? I don't want your parents coming in here again."

"Fine. Maybe Fek will forget about us and just take off. By sunrise he'll be halfway to Mars or wherever he wants to go. . ."

No reply from *The Spirit of St. Louis*.

I pulled the blankets up to my chin and lay there with my eyes wide open, staring into the darkness. I didn't want to die.

Like I was watching a movie, all the events of the past few days began passing through my mind.

The loud sound on Sunday night . . . the talking fire hydrant . . . Lauren Kyle's bravery when we burst into Mr. Pixley's barn . . .

. . . all the way to Fek's attack at school and tonight, when he'd sneaked into my room to do the brain probe.

And how had Fek been able to find me? Was he just smarter than Zymel?

And then . . .

Maybe during the brain probe, Fek had by accident given away information as well as getting it from me. Or perhaps my mind was just able to put together everything that had happened in the past few days.

Whatever it was, I knew.

I knew everything. I knew why the brain probe had been important to Fek, and I knew how frightened he was of me.

I knew where the spacecraft was hidden. Most important, I knew the shape Fek had taken to hide himself until his repairs were completed.

And if any proof were needed, it would take just a single telephone call.

I made the call the following morning, after Mom and Dad had left for work.

Bingo! I was right. It was proof enough even for Zymel.

After breakfast, I went outside to wait for Lauren and Dwight. Inside my book bag lay Zymel, shaped like the green book.

"Be ready for anything," I told him. "We may be having some fireworks in a little while."

"Frank, if you're keeping something from me . . ."

"Okay, Zymel, listen up. I haven't got much time."

Just then, Lauren walked out of her house. She joined me in the middle of the road.

"Lauren," I said, "maybe it'd be a good idea if you stayed home today."

"Why? I don't feel sick."

"Well . . . things might get kind of dangerous in a few minutes, and . . ."

"Hey, I didn't chicken out on you at the barn, did I? I've been right there with you during this whole mess with Zymel and Fek. Even when Zach and Corny came here yesterday, I stood by you, all the way."

"Sure, Lauren. But . . ."

"Well, I'm not running away now, Frank Dunn." She crossed her arms and nodded her head firmly. "Whatever's going to happen, I can put up as good a fight as you, any day."

Lauren was right. She'd done more than her share. And if Fek was out to kill, he'd come for her, too. She had a right to know everything I'd figured out. I started talking to her and Zymel in a low voice. Lauren's eyes got wider and wider as I told what I'd figured out last night.

"This is your idea, Frank," said Zymel. "You carry through on it, and Lauren and I will back you up. Just be careful. It could be dangerous and . . ."

He was interrupted by the front door of Dwight Hobisher's house banging open. We heard Mildew Beecham yelling like a fire siren.

"You get back here right after school, young man! I have some things I want you to . . ."

Dwight dashed outside, slammed the door behind

him, and bounded down the steps. "My folks'll be back from Washington in a few days," he said. "Then good-bye Mildew Beecham. I can hardly wait."

"Lucky you," I said. The three of us set off along the path to the bus stop.

Then I stopped walking and looked at my watch. "We've got a few minutes before the bus gets here," I told Dwight and Lauren. "Let's take a break."

"A break?" said Dwight.

"Yeah. Something's been happening this week to Lauren and me, and I think you should know about it."

"D'you really want to tell him . . ." Lauren began.

"Sure. Dwight's my buddy. And buddies don't have secrets. Y'see, Dwight, last Sunday I woke up in the middle of the night and . . ."

I quickly outlined all the things that had happened since Sunday. Lauren threw in a few remarks to cover things I'd forgotten.

Dwight stared at us as if we both had a screw loose somewhere. Maybe we did. But I knew . . .

"The only person who's around here all day and can keep an eye on things," I said, "is ol' Mildew Beecham. I think she ought to know about this."

"And I think you should both have your heads examined," said Dwight. "Of all the crazy . . . Hey, if all this is true, how come you didn't let me in on it? Aren't the three of us friends?"

"Zymel didn't want us to," said Lauren. "He's kind of our chief."

"Gee, thanks for leaving me out in the cold," Dwight replied. "But if you think Mildew can help, I'll tell her the whole screwy yarn as soon as I get home from school. She'll say I'm nuts, but . . ."

"Maybe we shouldn't wait that long, Dwight," I told him. "Things could be happening around here while we're at school. Let's go back now and . . ."

"I'll go, Frank. Tell the bus driver to wait for me."

I looked straight at Lauren and began talking to her as if Dwight wasn't anywhere around. "Funny thing, Lauren. All week long, we haven't seen Mildew, even once. Oh sure, we've heard her screaming at Dwight from inside the house. But today I'd like to look her in the eye. Come on. Let's us two go back."

"Sure, Frank," she said. "Dwight, you tell the bus driver to wait for us."

"Don't go getting Mildew all upset just because . . ."

But Lauren and I were already walking back along the path.

"Wait a minute," Dwight called after us. "I'll come with you."

"No, Dwight," I said. I put down my book bag. "You stay right where you are. Don't come a step closer."

"You two are acting like a couple of lunatics. What do you think is going on here?"

"We *know* what's going on," said Lauren grimly. She bent down and unzipped the cover of my book bag.

"A couple of days ago," I told Dwight, "Fek the criminal was in school, looking for tools. Why was he at school? I asked myself. Why didn't he go to a hardware store or a factory?"

"Why?" Dwight repeated.

"Because the thing that was his disguise had to be in school to avoid suspicion," I answered. "Then, after I'd seen Fek in the custodian's shop, he had to know how much *I* knew. So he came into my room last night to do a brain probe while I was asleep. But I woke up and discovered him."

"Where do you figure this Fek thing is now, Frank?"

"Not far away at all, Dwight."

Dwight looked around as if he was puzzled.

"Oh, cut that out!" Lauren snapped at him. "It's all over."

"What's all over?"

"Everything, Dwight," said Lauren. "Or should we call you Fek?"

Dwight just stared at us and shook his head sadly. "Maybe it's something in the drinking water," he sighed. "Both of you have rotting brains."

"Oh no, Dwight," I said. "You're all through."

"Ask me anything you want to. I'll prove I'm . . ."

"Sure you will. Because you did a brain probe of the real Dwight Hobisher while he was asleep last Sunday, so you've got all the information that was in his mind. You knew Mildew Beecham wouldn't be out here this week. But you convinced Lauren and me that she was staying at your house by imitating her voice, screaming at you.

"Maybe the fact that nobody ever *saw* Mildew was my first tip-off. Getting her body and her clothes just right would be too complicated, even for a shape-changer."

"But . . ."

"The way things were," Lauren went on, "you had lots of time in your house alone. You could put the spacecraft in your garage. Plenty of room, and no visitors because everybody was scared of your imitation of Mildew."

"Everything went along fine for a while," I added. "But then I ran into you at school, in the shape of Mr. Follett. How close were Zymel and I to discovering where you'd hidden the ship? You had to know. So you sneaked into my room last night and . . ."

"And this is about as dumb as anything I've ever listened to," said Dwight. "Frank . . . Lauren . . . If you could hear yourselves, you'd know you're talking like a couple of jerks."

"Tell him, Frank," said Lauren. "Tell him where the *real* Dwight Hobisher is."

"Last Sunday afternoon," I said, "*before* the spaceship crashed, Dwight told me his parents would be staying at the Federalist Hotel in Washington, D.C. D'you recognize that name, Fek?"

"I'm not Fek, you jerk. I'm Dwight. And of course I recognize the name. Mom and Dad always use that hotel when they're in Washington."

"Yeah? Well, I phoned the Federalist Hotel about half an hour ago. The guy at the desk rang up the Hobishers' room. And who should answer but Dwight himself. So, since the real Dwight's in Washington, you have to be . . ."

Whish!

What had been Dwight Hobisher's form suddenly began to twist and expand. There was a loud sound of cloth tearing as the thing ripped its way out of the clothes it wore.

There before me was a monstrous creature nearly eight feet high, with a leathery body and two great alligatorlike heads.

Fek—for the thing had to be Fek—bent toward me. From both mouths, hot breath steamed against my face. The great teeth came nearer and nearer.

Suddenly a rock struck the nearest head with a thump. The head turned toward Lauren, who'd already picked up another rock.

With jaws gaping, the head reached out for Lauren. "Zymel!" she screamed. "Help me!"

Out of my book bag sprang what seemed to be a snake. But who ever heard of a snake as big around as a barrel, or one that moved about on hundreds of furry, pawed legs? Suddenly both of Fek's alligator heads turned toward the weird creature.

"Leave the boy and girl alone, Fek." It was Zymel's voice that came from the snake's mouth. "This fight is between you and me."

"I'll do battle in whatever way will make me the winner," hissed one alligator head.

"No bi-brain has ever defeated a Salurian milli-serpent."

Whish!

A bat-thing nearly as tall as a man took the place of the first monster. The great bat flew at the snake-creature. The legged snake retreated. The bat swooped after it.

Whish!

Where the snake had been was now a huge red-and-black ball covered with wickedly sharp green spines. By expelling air from openings in its surface, the ball jetted toward the bat-thing, which squawked and dodged, avoiding contact with the spines.

Whish!

What thumped back to earth was no longer a bat.

Four powerful legs supported a body that was bulky and muscular. On top of the massive neck was a squat, flat head with curving horns on top of it.

The creature pawed the ground and squinted through red eyes at the place beneath a tree where Lauren and I were crouched.

"It's getting ready to charge," I whispered in a voice filled with fear.

Lauren looked up and called to the red-and-black ball that was Zymel to help us.

Suddenly the spiked ball disappeared.

Lauren and I were alone with Fek.

"Frank, run!" Lauren shouted.

"You run! I'm too scared!"

We looked about for a way to escape. The moment either Lauren or I made a move, the monster Fek scurried to cut us off.

It began slowly stalking us, forcing us further and further back. It moved one way, then another, making us retreat in the direction it chose.

Finally our backs were against a big maple tree. Thirty feet away, the creature opened its mouth.

"I will butt your soft bodies into jelly," said Fek's voice, menacingly.

"But Zymel will . . ." Lauren began.

"Zymel will do nothing. Did you see how he fled, once I became a Konsiglian ram? The ram is a creature that can stand up to any other living thing.

Nothing can defeat it."

The head lowered. The powerful legs stomped and pawed at the earth. The horns were like the pointed ends of a living battering ram.

The beast lurched toward us, gaining speed at every step. Finally the legs were a blur as the body approached like an express train. The lowered head seemed to get larger and larger, and when it smashed against our fragile bones, we would . . .

Whish!

All at once we couldn't see the ram anymore. Something had come between it and us. At almost the same instant, I heard a thud, like a gigantic sledgehammer striking a chunk of knotty oak wood.

Then . . . silence.

Lauren and I stared at the great boulder that had suddenly appeared in front of us, right in the path of Fek's charge.

As we watched, a pair of lips suddenly sprouted out of the surface of the huge rock.

"Not bad, huh?" said the lips.

"Zymel? Is that you?"

"Of course. When I saw that Fek had become a Konsiglian ram, I knew I couldn't best him in the form of some other creature. So I changed into a tiny gnat and bided my time until he got ready to charge. Then I placed myself between you two and took this shape."

We looked at the spot where the gigantic ram beast was lying limply, with its eyes closed.

"And Fek is . . ." I began.

"Even a Konsiglian ram can't run full-tilt into a boulder without sustaining some damage," said Zymel.

"You did it, Zymel," I said. "You captured Fek."

"No," came the reply. "*We* did it. Frank, if you hadn't discovered that Fek was hiding in Dwight's body . . ."

"Ah, you'd have figured it out eventually, Zymel. Maybe if you tried sleeping a little more often than once very four days . . ."

"Hey!" Lauren cried out. "What about me? I was out there too, putting my neck on the line."

"You can say that again," I told her. "If you hadn't thrown the rock at that first monster, I'd have been nothing more than something it ate for lunch."

"And don't forget about how I broke in the door of the barn the other night," Lauren said. "And lent Mary Farr my clothes and . . ."

"You are both to be commended," said Zymel. "No one in the whole Rodinam police force could have performed more diligently or bravely."

"How about that?" said Lauren, looking down at me. "We're a couple of heroes."

"And if either Zach Baylor or Corny Cobb lays a hand on me again, I'm gonna slug 'em both, right between the eyes," I said. "If I can face a Konsiglian ram, I can stand up to anything!"

"Watch out, everybody!" Lauren crowed. "Whether you're at Rolling Acres or Rodinam, here come the good guys. Me and Frank!"

After all this excitement, going to school was out of the question. Zymel turned back into his real form and oozed his way to the unconscious ram. He covered the animal's head with a cap of gray jelly.

Suddenly the ram's eyes popped open. It staggered to its feet and glared at me through red-rimmed eyes.

I got all shaky and looked around for someplace to hide. But then I heard Zymel's calm voice coming from the blob on the monster's head.

"It's quite safe now. I am in control of all of Fek's actions. He cannot exercise his own will until I release him."

We headed back toward home. The great ram trotted beside me, as tame as a kitten.

When we got to the Hobisher house, I had to break a window in the back door to get us inside. We searched all over, but as we suspected, there was no sign that Mildew Beecham had ever been there.

But sure enough, there in the garage was the ship, looking a bit like a gigantic silver wheel. Zymel spoke some strange-sounding words. A door in the ship's side slid open.

"Now to tend to my prisoner," said Zymel. "First I'll make him assume his own shape."

Zymel's gray body began to throb. At the same time, the monster ram started to melt away. In its place was a second blob—this one of pale yellow.

Zymel hauled the yellow blob inside the ship. There was a soft humming, and tiny lights appeared at the little windows.

Zymel came to the door again. "All seems to be in order," he told Lauren and me. "The power system is operative, and I have locked Fek into the ion cell again. But we were just in time. He has completed nearly all the repairs."

For the next couple of hours, Lauren and I handed tools through the ship's door in to Zymel. Finally the shape-changer appeared and pronounced the ship ready to go.

"It is the time of parting," he said. "And I shall miss you both. I have no medals or awards that I can give you. You will find, I'm afraid, that few if any will believe what you have seen and done these past few days. But your names will be listed among the heroes of my planet, Rodinam."

I never thought I'd get all weepy over a blob of gelatin with an eye in it. But I felt a tear roll down my cheek.

"And when you—or your descendants—discover the means to travel to Rodinam," Zymel went on, "the most joyous and wonderful welcome will be extended. You may depend on it. Frank . . . Lauren . . . you are brave and you are intelligent, and you are a tribute to the many forms of life that make up our universe. I am proud to call you my friends."

The eye within the gray blob blinked twice. Then the blob disappeared and the ship's door slammed shut.

There was a humming sound that got louder and louder. All at once the ship rose into the air.

I punched a button on the wall. The garage door rolled open.

Lauren and I watched the ship as it glided outside. It rose straight up.

Suddenly it shot off through the sky, faster than our eyes could follow.

Then . . . it was gone.